CLASSIC STORIES
OF THE SEA

More short stories available
from Macmillan Collector's Library

CLASSIC STORIES
OF THE SEA

Selection and introduction by
HARRIET SANDERS

MACMILLAN COLLECTOR'S LIBRARY

This collection first published 2024 by Macmillan Collector's Library
an imprint of Pan Macmillan
The Smithson, 6 Briset Street, London ECIM 5NR
EU representative: Macmillan Publishers Ireland Ltd, 1st Floor,
The Liffey Trust Centre, 117–126 Sheriff Street Upper,
Dublin 1, DOI YC43
Associated companies throughout the world
www.panmacmillan.com

ISBN 978-1-0350-1492-7

1 3 5 7 9 8 6 4 2

A CIP catalogue record for this book is available from the British Library.

Casing design and endpaper pattern by Andrew Davidson
Typeset in Plantin by Jouve (UK), Milton Keynes
Printed and bound in China by Imago

Visit **www.panmacmillan.com** to read more
about all our books and to buy them.

To Robert

Contents

Preface

HARRIET SANDERS

Maritime literature, a genre that captures the enduring bond between humans and the sea, rose to prominence in the late nineteenth and early twentieth centuries. The sea – vast, formidable and unpredictable – inspired writers like Joseph Conrad, Rudyard Kipling, Jack London and Stephen Crane to write powerful stories about the allure and the danger of life at sea.

Here are tales of adventure in which a vivid cast of seafarers must pit their wits against fierce oceans, terrifying storms and creatures of the deep. But these are not mere imaginative inventions. The majority of writers included in this collection drew on their own maritime experience, lending the stories a magnificent authenticity. Jack London was famous for his sea voyages, friends Joseph Conrad and Perceval Gibbon both served in the British Royal Navy, and it's no surprise that J. F. Wilson's 'Ninety Days' is so convincing given his own long service at sea.

Man versus the elements offers a fertile backdrop to tackle a wide range of themes. Many stories focus on the tension between endurance and moral ambiguity. While Crane's account of a terrible shipwreck, 'The Open Boat', highlights the resilience of the human spirit against the very worst that nature – overpowering and indifferent – can throw at it, Jack London's 'Make Westing' is a tale of courage that tips into obsession when setting the right course in the most dangerous of seas takes precedence over everything. In extreme and isolated conditions, human nature is tested to the limit and, at sea, normal rules don't always apply.

Life at sea also, of course, inspired great loyalty and a sense of duty, which is beautifully portrayed in stories such as 'The Captain's Arm' by Perceval Gibbons, in which a retired captain saves the day when he takes control of his drunken son's ship. And J. F. Wilson's 'Ninety Days' celebrates themes of loyalty, perseverance and camaraderie.

Enjoy this rich and varied collection for its vivid evocation of life at sea, for its exploration of very relevant issues of struggle, survival, resilience and moral uncertainty, but, most of all, enjoy it for the thrill of adventure.

Rudyard Kipling

A Matter of Fact

And if ye doubt the tale I tell,
Steer through the South Pacific swell;
Go where the branching coral hives
Unending strife of endless lives,
Where, leagued about the 'wildered boat,
The rainbow jellies fill and float;
And, lilting where the laver lingers,
The starfish trips on all her fingers;
Where, 'neath his myriad spines ashock,
The sea-egg ripples down the rock;
An orange wonder dimly guessed,
From darkness where the cuttles rest,
Moored o'er the darker deeps that hide
The blind white Sea-snake and his bride
Who, drowsing, nose the long-lost ships
Let down through darkness to their lips.

The Palms.

Once a priest, always a priest; once a mason, always a mason; but once a journalist, always and for ever a journalist.

There were three of us, all newspaper men, the

only passengers on a little tramp steamer that ran where her owners told her to go. She had once been in the Bilbao iron ore business, had been lent to the Spanish Government for service at Manilla; and was ending her days in the Cape Town coolie-trade, with occasional trips to Madagascar and even as far as England. We found her going to Southampton in ballast, and shipped in her because the fares were nominal. There was Keller, of an American paper, on his way back to the States from palace executions in Madagascar; there was a burly half-Dutchman, called Zuyland, who owned and edited a paper up country near Johannesburg; and there was myself, who had solemnly put away all journalism, vowing to forget that I had ever known the difference between an imprint and a stereo advertisement.

Ten minutes after Keller spoke to me, as the *Rathmines* cleared Cape Town, I had forgotten the aloofness I desired to feign, and was in heated discussion on the immorality of expanding telegrams beyond a certain fixed point. Then Zuyland came out of his cabin, and we were all at home instantly, because we were men of the same profession needing no introduction. We annexed the boat formally, broke open the passengers' bath-room door—on the Manilla lines the Dons do not wash—cleaned out the orange-peel and cigar-ends at the bottom of the bath, hired a Lascar to shave us throughout the voyage, and then asked each other's names.

Three ordinary men would have quarrelled through sheer boredom before they reached Southampton. We, by virtue of our craft, were anything but ordinary men. A large percentage of the tales of the world, the thirty-nine that cannot be told to ladies and the one that can, are common property coming of a common stock. We told them all, as a matter of form, with all their local and specific variants which are surprising. Then came, in the intervals of steady card-play, more personal histories of adventure and things seen and suffered: panics among white folk, when the blind terror ran from man to man on the Brooklyn Bridge, and the people crushed each other to death they knew not why; fires, and faces that opened and shut their mouths horribly at red-hot window frames; wrecks in frost and snow, reported from the sleet-sheathed rescue-tug at the risk of frostbite; long rides after diamond thieves; skirmishes on the veldt and in municipal committees with the Boers; glimpses of lazy tangled Cape politics and the mule-rule in the Transvaal; card-tales, horse-tales, woman-tales, by the score and the half hundred; till the first mate, who had seen more than us all put together, but lacked words to clothe his tales with, sat open-mouthed far into the dawn.

When the tales were done we picked up cards till a curious hand or a chance remark made one or other of us say, 'That reminds me of a man who—or a business which—' and the anecdotes would continue while the *Rathmines* kicked her way northward through the warm water.

In the morning of one specially warm night we three were sitting immediately in front of the wheelhouse, where an old Swedish boatswain whom we called 'Frithiof the Dane' was at the wheel, pretending that he could not hear our stories. Once or twice Frithiof spun the spokes curiously, and Keller lifted his head from a long chair to ask, 'What is it? Can't you get any steerageway on her?'

'There is a feel in the water,' said Frithiof, 'that I cannot understand. I think that we run downhills or somethings. She steers bad this morning.'

Nobody seems to know the laws that govern the pulse of the big waters. Sometimes even a landsman can tell that the solid ocean is atilt, and that the ship is working herself up a long unseen slope; and sometimes the captain says, when neither full steam nor fair wind justifies the length of a day's run, that the ship is sagging downhill; but how these ups and downs come about has not yet been settled authoritatively.

4

'No, it is a following sea,' said Frithiof; 'and with a following sea you shall not get good steerage-way.'

The sea was as smooth as a duck-pond, except for a regular oily swell. As I looked over the side to see where it might be following us from, the sun rose in a perfectly clear sky and struck the water with its light so sharply that it seemed as though the sea should clang like a burnished gong. The wake of the screw and the little white streak cut by the log-line hanging over the stern were the only marks on the water as far as eye could reach.

Keller rolled out of his chair and went aft to get a pine-apple from the ripening stock that was hung inside the after awning.

'Frithiof, the log-line has got tired of swimming. It's coming home,' he drawled.

'What?' said Frithiof, his voice jumping several octaves.

'Coming home,' Keller repeated, leaning over the stern. I ran to his side and saw the log-line, which till then had been drawn tense over the stern railing, slacken, loop, and come up off the port quarter. Frithiof called up the speaking-tube to the bridge, and the bridge answered, 'Yes, nine knots.' Then Frithiof spoke again, and the answer was, 'What do you want of the skipper?' and Frithiof bellowed, 'Call him up.'

By this time Zuyland, Keller, and myself had caught something of Frithiof's excitement, for any emotion on shipboard is most contagious. The captain ran out of his cabin, spoke to Frithiof, looked at the log-line, jumped on the bridge, and in a minute we felt the steamer swing round as Frithiof turned her.

''Going back to Cape Town?' said Keller.

Frithiof did not answer, but tore away at the wheel. Then he beckoned us three to help, and we held the wheel down till the *Rathmines* answered it, and we found ourselves looking into the white of our own wake, with the still oily sea tearing past our bows, though we were not going more than half steam ahead.

The captain stretched out his arm from the bridge and shouted. A minute later I would have given a great deal to have shouted too, for one-half of the sea seemed to shoulder itself above the other half, and came on in the shape of a hill. There was neither crest, comb, nor curl-over to it; nothing but black water with little waves chasing each other about the flanks. I saw it stream past and on a level with the *Rathmines*' bow-plates before the steamer hove up her bulk to rise, and I argued that this would be the last of all earthly voyages for me. Then we lifted for ever and ever and ever, till I heard

Keller saying in my ear, 'The bowels of the deep, good Lord!' and the *Rathmines* stood poised, her screw racing and drumming on the slope of a hollow that stretched downwards for a good half-mile.

We went down that hollow, nose under for the most part, and the air smelt wet and muddy, like that of an emptied aquarium. There was a second hill to climb; I saw that much: but the water came aboard and carried me aft till it jammed me against the wheel-house door, and before I could catch breath or clear my eyes again we were rolling to and fro in torn water, with the scuppers pouring like eaves in a thunderstorm.

'There were three waves,' said Keller; 'and the stokehold's flooded.'

The firemen were on deck waiting, apparently, to be drowned. The engineer came and dragged them below, and the crew, gasping, began to work the clumsy Board of Trade pump. That showed nothing serious, and when I understood that the *Rathmines* was really on the water, and not beneath it, I asked what had happened.

'The captain says it was a blow-up under the sea—a volcano,' said Keller.

'It hasn't warmed anything,' I said. I was feeling bitterly cold, and cold was almost unknown in those waters. I went below to change my clothes, and when I came up everything was wiped out in cling-ing white fog.

'Are there going to be any more surprises?' said Keller to the captain.

'I don't know. Be thankful you're alive, gentle-men. That's a tidal wave thrown up by a volcano. Probably the bottom of the sea has been lifted a few feet somewhere or other. I can't quite understand this cold spell. Our sea-thermometer says the sur-face water is 44° and it should be 68° at least.'

'It's abominable,' said Keller, shivering. 'But hadn't you better attend to the fog-horn? It seems to me that I heard something.'

'Heard! Good heavens!' said the captain from the bridge, 'I should think you did.' He pulled the string of our fog-horn, which was a weak one. It sputtered and choked, because the stokehold was full of water and the fires were half-drowned, and at last gave out a moan. It was answered from the fog by one of the most appalling steam-sirens I have ever heard. Keller turned as white as I did, for the fog, the cold fog, was upon us, and any man may be forgiven for fearing a death he cannot see.

'Give her steam there!' said the captain to the engine-room. 'Steam for the whistle, if we have to go dead slow.'

We bellowed again, and the damp dripped off the

awnings on to the deck as we listened for the reply. It seemed to be astern this time, but much nearer than before.

'The *Pembroke Castle* on us!' said Keller; and then, viciously, 'Well, thank God, we shall sink her too.'

'It's a side-wheel steamer,' I whispered. 'Can't you hear the paddles?'

This time we whistled and roared till the steam gave out, and the answer nearly deafened us. There was a sound of frantic threshing in the water, apparently about fifty yards away, and something shot past in the whiteness that looked as though it were gray and red.

'The *Pembroke Castle* bottom up,' said Keller, who, being a journalist, always sought for explanations. 'That's the colours of a Castle liner. We're in for a big thing.'

'The sea is bewitched,' said Frithiof from the wheel-house. 'There are *two* steamers!'

Another siren sounded on our bow, and the little steamer rolled in the wash of something that had passed unseen.

'We're evidently in the middle of a fleet,' said Keller quietly. 'If one doesn't run us down, the other will. Phew! What in creation is that?'

I sniffed, for there was a poisonous rank smell in the cold air—a smell that I had smelt before.

'If I was on land I should say that it was an alligator. It smells like musk,' I answered.

'Not ten thousand alligators could make that smell,' said Zuyland; 'I have smelt them.'

'Bewitched! Bewitched!' said Frithiof. 'The sea she is turned upside down, and we are walking along the bottom.'

Again the *Rathmines* rolled in the wash of some unseen ship, and a silver-gray wave broke over the bow, leaving on the deck a sheet of sediment—the gray broth that has its place in the fathomless deeps of the sea. A sprinkling of the wave fell on my face, and it was so cold that it stung as boiling water stings. The dead and most untouched deep water of the sea had been heaved to the top by the submarine volcano—the chill still water that kills all life and smells of desolation and emptiness. We did not need either the blinding fog or that indescribable smell of musk to make us unhappy—we were shivering with cold and wretchedness where we stood.

'The hot air on the cold water makes this fog,' said the captain; 'it ought to clear in a little time.'

'Whistle, oh! whistle, and let's get out of it,' said Keller.

The captain whistled again, and far and far astern the invisible twin steam-sirens answered us. Their blasting shriek grew louder, till at last it seemed to tear out of the fog just above our quarter, and I cowered while the *Rathmines* plunged bows under on a double swell that crossed.

'No more,' said Frithiof, 'it is not good any more. Let us get away, in the name of God.'

'Now if a torpedo-boat with a *City of Paris* siren went mad and broke her moorings and hired a friend to help her, it's just conceivable that we might be carried as we are now. Otherwise this thing is—'

The last words died on Keller's lips, his eyes began to start from his head, and his jaw fell. Some six or seven feet above the port bulwarks, framed in fog, and as utterly unsupported as the full moon, hung a Face. It was not human, and it certainly was not animal, for it did not belong to this earth as known to man. The mouth was open, revealing a ridiculously tiny tongue—as absurd as the tongue of an elephant; there were tense wrinkles of white skin at the angles of the drawn lips, white feelers like those of a barbel sprung from the lower jaw, and there was no sign of teeth within the mouth. But the horror of the face lay in the eyes, for those were sightless—white, in sockets as white as scraped bone, and blind. Yet for all this the face, wrinkled as the mask of a lion is drawn in Assyrian sculpture, was alive with rage and terror. One long white feeler touched our bulwarks. Then the face disappeared with the swiftness of a blindworm popping into its burrow, and the next thing that I remember is my own voice in my own ears, saying gravely to the mainmast, 'But the air-bladder ought to have been forced out of its mouth, you know.'

Keller came up to me, ashy white. He put his hand into his pocket, took a cigar, bit it, dropped it, thrust his shaking thumb into his mouth and mumbled, 'The giant gooseberry and the raining frogs! Gimme a light—gimme a light! Say, gimme a light.' A little bead of blood dropped from his thumb-joint.

I respected the motive, though the manifestation was absurd. 'Stop, you'll bite your thumb off,' I said, and Keller laughed brokenly as he picked up his cigar. Only Zuyland, leaning over the port bulwarks, seemed self-possessed. He declared later that he was very sick.

'We've seen it,' he said, turning round. 'That is it.'

'What?' said Keller, chewing the unlighted cigar.

As he spoke the fog was blown into shreds, and we saw the sea, gray with mud, rolling on every side of us and empty of all life. Then in one spot it bubbled and became like the pot of ointment that the Bible speaks of. From that wide-ringed trouble a Thing came up—a gray and red Thing with a neck—a Thing that bellowed and writhed in pain. Frithiof drew in his breath and held it till the red letters of the ship's name, woven across his jersey, straggled and opened out as though they had been type badly set. Then he said with a little cluck in his throat, 'Ah me! It is blind. *Hur illa!* That thing is blind,' and a murmur of pity went through us all, for we could see that the thing on the water was blind and in pain. Something had gashed and cut the great sides cruelly and the blood was spurting out. The gray ooze of the undermost sea lay in the monstrous wrinkles of the back, and poured away in sluices. The blind white head flung back and battered the wounds, and the body in its torment rose clear of the red and gray waves till we saw a pair of quivering shoulders streaked with weed and rough with shells, but as white in the clear spaces as the hairless, maneless, blind, toothless head. Afterwards, came a dot on the horizon and the sound of a shrill scream, and it was as though a shuttle shot all across the sea in one breath, and a second head and neck tore through the levels, driving a whispering wall of water to right and left. The two Things met—the one untouched and the other in its death-throe—male and female, we said, the female coming to the male. She circled round him bellowing, and laid her neck across the curve of his great turtle-back, and he disappeared under water for an instant, but flung up again, grunting in agony while the blood ran. Once the entire head and neck shot clear of the water and stiffened, and I heard Keller saying, as though he was watching a street accident, 'Give him air. For God's sake, give him air.' Then the death-struggle began, with crampings and twistings and jerkings of the white bulk to and fro, till our little steamer rolled again, and each gray wave coated her plates with the gray slime. The sun was clear, there was no wind, and we watched, the whole crew, stokers and all, in wonder and pity, but chiefly pity. The Thing was so helpless, and, save for his mate, so alone. No human eye should have beheld him; it was monstrous and indecent to exhibit him there in trade waters between atlas degrees of latitude. He had been spewed up, mangled and dying, from his rest on the sea-floor, where he might have lived till the Judgment Day, and we saw the tides of his life go from him as an angry tide goes out across rocks in the teeth of a landward gale. His mate lay rocking on the water a little distance off, bellowing continually, and the smell of musk came down upon the ship making us cough.

At last the battle for life ended in a batter of coloured seas. We saw the writhing neck fall like a flail, the carcase turn sideways, showing the glint of a white belly and the inset of a gigantic hind leg or flipper. Then all sank, and sea boiled over it, while the mate swam round and round, darting her head in every direction. Though we might have feared that she would attack the steamer, no power on earth could have drawn anyone of us from our places that hour. We watched, holding our breaths. The mate paused in her search; we could hear the wash beating along her sides; reared her neck as high as she could reach, blind and lonely in all that loneliness of the sea, and sent one desperate bellow booming across the swells as an oyster-shell skips across a pond. Then she made off to the westward, the sun shining on the white head and the wake behind it, till nothing was left to see but a little pin point of silver on the horizon. We stood on our course again; and the *Rathmines*, coated with the sea-sediment from bow to stern, looked like a ship made gray with terror.

'We must pool our notes,' was the first coherent remark from Keller. 'We're three trained journalists— we hold absolutely the biggest scoop on record. Start fair.'

I objected to this. Nothing is gained by collaboration in journalism when all deal with the same facts, so we went to work each according to his own lights. Keller triple-headed his account, talked about our 'gallant captain,' and wound up with an allusion to American enterprise in that it was a citizen of

Dayton, Ohio, that had seen the sea-serpent. This sort of thing would have discredited the Creation, much more a mere sea tale, but as a specimen of the picture-writing of a half-civilised people it was very interesting. Zuyland took a heavy column and a half, giving approximate lengths and breadths, and the whole list of the crew whom he had sworn on oath to testify to his facts. There was nothing fantastic or flamboyant in Zuyland. I wrote three-quarters of a leaded bourgeois column, roughly speaking, and refrained from putting any journalese into it for reasons that had begun to appear to me.

Keller was insolent with joy. He was going to cable from Southampton to the New York *World*, mail his account to America on the same day, paralyse London with his three columns of loosely knitted headlines, and generally efface the earth. 'You'll see how I work a big scoop when I get it,' he said.

'Is this your first visit to England?' I asked.

'Yes,' said he. 'You don't seem to appreciate the beauty of our scoop. It's pyramidal—the death of the sea-serpent! Good heavens alive, man, it's the biggest thing ever vouchsafed to a paper!'

'Curious to think that it will never appear in any paper, isn't it?' I said.

Zuyland was near me, and he nodded quickly.

'What do you mean?' said Keller. 'If you're enough of a Britisher to throw this thing away, I shan't. I thought you were a newspaperman.'

'I am. That's why I know. Don't be an ass, Keller. Remember, I'm seven hundred years your senior, and what your grandchildren may learn five hundred years hence, I learned from my grandfathers about five hundred years ago. You won't do it, because you can't.'

This conversation was held in open sea, where everything seems possible, some hundred miles from Southampton. We passed the Needles Light at dawn, and the lifting day showed the stucco villas on the green and the awful orderliness of England—line upon line, wall upon wall, solid stone dock and monolithic pier. We waited an hour in the Customs shed, and there was ample time for the effect to soak in.

'Now, Keller, you face the music. The *Havel* goes out to-day. Mail by her, and I'll take you to the telegraph-office,' I said.

I heard Keller gasp as the influence of the land closed about him, cowing him as they say Newmarket Heath cows a young horse unused to open courses.

'I want to retouch my stuff. Suppose we wait till we get to London?' he said.

Zuyland, by the way, had torn up his account and thrown it overboard that morning early. His reasons were my reasons.

In the train Keller began to revise his copy, and every time that he looked at the trim little fields, the red villas, and the embankments of the line, the blue pencil plunged remorselessly through the slips. He appeared to have dredged the dictionary for adjectives. I could think of none that he had not used. Yet he was a perfectly sound poker-player and never showed more cards than were sufficient to take the pool.

'Aren't you going to leave him a single bellow?' I asked sympathetically. 'Remember, everything goes in the States, from a trouser-button to a double-eagle.'

'That's just the curse of it,' said Keller below his breath. 'We've played 'em for suckers so often that when it comes to the golden truth—I'd like to try this on a London paper. You have first call there, though.'

'Not in the least. I'm not touching the thing in our papers. I shall be happy to leave 'em all to you; but surely you'll cable it home?'

'No. Not if I can make the scoop here and see the Britishers sit up.'

'You won't do it with three columns of slushy

headline, believe me. They don't sit up as quickly as some people.'

'I'm beginning to think that too. Does *nothing* make any difference in this country?' he said, looking out of the window. 'How old is that farmhouse?'

'New. It can't be more than two hundred years at the most.'

'Um. Fields, too?'

'That hedge there must have been clipped for about eighty years.'

'Labour cheap—eh?'

'Pretty much. Well, I suppose you'd like to try the *Times*, wouldn't you?'

'No,' said Keller, looking at Winchester Cathedral. ''Might as well try to electrify a haystack. And to think that the *World* would take three columns and ask for more—with illustrations too! It's sickening.'

'But the *Times* might,' I began.

Keller flung his paper across the carriage, and it opened in its austere majesty of solid type—opened with the crackle of an encyclopaedia.

'Might! You *might* work your way through the bow-plates of a cruiser. Look at that first page!'

'It strikes you that way, does it?' I said. 'Then I'd recommend you to try a light and frivolous journal.'

'With a thing like this of mine—of ours? It's sacred history!'

I showed him a paper which I conceived would be after his own heart, in that it was modelled on American lines.

'That's homey, 'he said, 'but it's not the real thing. Now, I should like one of these fat old *Times* columns. Probably there'd be a bishop in the office, though.'

When we reached London Keller disappeared in the direction of the Strand. What his experiences may have been I cannot tell, but it seems that he invaded the office of an evening paper at 11.45 a.m. (I told him English editors were most idle at that hour), and mentioned my name as that of a witness to the truth of his story.

'I was nearly fired out,' he said furiously at lunch. 'As soon as I mentioned you, the old man said that I was to tell you that they didn't want any more of your practical jokes, and that you knew the hours to call if you had anything to sell, and that they'd see you condemned before they helped to puff one of your infernal yarns in advance. Say, what record do you hold for truth in this country, anyway?'

'A beauty. You ran up against it, that's all. Why don't you leave the English papers alone and cable to New York? Everything goes over there.'

'Can't you see that's just why?' he repeated.

'I saw it a long time ago. You don't intend to cable, then?'

'Yes, I do,' he answered, in the over-emphatic voice of one who does not know his own mind.

That afternoon I walked him abroad and about, over the streets that run between the pavements like channels of grooved and tongued lava, over the bridges that are made of enduring stone, through subways floored and sided with yard-thick concrete, between houses that are never rebuilt, and by river-steps hewn, to the eye, from the living rock. A black fog chased us into Westminster Abbey, and, standing there in the darkness, I could hear the wings of the dead centuries circling round the head of Litchfield A. Keller, journalist, of Dayton, Ohio, U.S.A., whose mission it was to make the Britishers sit up.

He stumbled gasping into the thick gloom, and the roar of the traffic came to his bewildered ears.

'Let's go to the telegraph-office and cable,' I said. 'Can't you hear the New York *World* crying for news of the great sea-serpent, blind, white, and smelling of musk, stricken to death by a submarine volcano, and assisted by his loving wife to die in mid-ocean, as visualised by an American citizen, the breezy, newsy, brainy newspaper man of Dayton, Ohio? 'Rah for the Buckeye State. Step lively! Both gates! Szz! Boom!

Aah!' Keller was a Princeton man, and he seemed to need encouragement.

'You've got me on your own ground,' said he, tugging at his overcoat pocket. He pulled out his copy, with the cable forms—for he had written out his telegram—and put them all into my hand, groaning, 'I pass. If I hadn't come to your cursed country—If I'd sent it off at Southampton—If I ever get you west of the Alleghannies, if—'

'Never mind, Keller. It isn't your fault. It's the fault of your country. If you had been seven hundred years older you'd have done what I am going to do.'

'What are you going to do?'

'Tell it as a lie.'

'Fiction?' This with the full-blooded disgust of a journalist for the illegitimate branch of the profession.

'You can call it that if you like. I shall call it a lie.'

And a lie it has become; for Truth is a naked lady, and if by accident she is drawn up from the bottom of the sea, it behoves a gentleman either to give her a print petticoat or to turn his face to the wall and vow that he did not see.

STEPHEN CRANE

The Open Boat

I

None of them knew the color of the sky. Their eyes glanced level, and were fastened upon the waves that swept toward them. These waves were of the hue of slate, save for the tops, which were of foaming white, and all of the men knew the colors of the sea. The horizon narrowed and widened, and dipped and rose, and at all times its edge was jagged with waves that seemed thrust up in points like rocks.

Many a man ought to have a bath-tub larger than the boat which here rode upon the sea. These waves were most wrongfully and barbarously abrupt and tall, and each froth-top was a problem in small-boat navigation.

The cook squatted in the bottom, and looked with both eyes at the six inches of gunwale which separated him from the ocean. His sleeves were rolled over his fat forearms, and the two flaps of his unbuttoned vest dangled as he bent to bail out the boat. Often he said, "Gawd! that was a narrow clip." As he remarked it he invariably gazed eastward over the broken sea.

The oiler, steering with one of the two oars in the boat, sometimes raised himself suddenly to keep clear of water that swirled in over the stern. It was a thin little oar, and it seemed often ready to snap.

The correspondent, pulling at the other oar, watched the waves and wondered why he was there.

The injured captain, lying in the bow, was at this time buried in that profound dejection and indifference which comes, temporarily at least, to even the bravest and most enduring when, willy-nilly, the firm fails, the army loses, the ship goes down. The mind of the master of a vessel is rooted deep in the timbers of her, though he command for a day or a decade; and this captain had on him the stern impression of a scene in the grays of dawn of seven turned faces, and later a stump of a topmast with a white ball on it, that slashed to and fro at the waves, went low and lower, and down. Thereafter there was something strange in his voice. Although steady, it was deep with mourning, and of a quality beyond oration or tears.

"Keep 'er a little more south, Billie," said he.

"A little more south, sir," said the oiler in the stern.

A seat in this boat was not unlike a seat upon a bucking broncho, and, by the same token, a broncho is not much smaller. The craft pranced and reared and plunged like an animal. As each wave came, and she rose for it, she seemed like a horse making at a fence outrageously high. The manner of her scramble over these walls of water is a mystic thing, and, moreover, at the top of them were ordinarily these problems in white water, the foam racing down from the summit of each wave, requiring a new leap, and a leap from the air. Then, after scornfully bumping a crest, she would slide and race and splash down a long incline, and arrive bobbing and nodding in front of the next menace.

A singular disadvantage of the sea lies in the fact that, after successfully surmounting one wave, you discover that there is another behind it, just as important and just as nervously anxious to do something effective in the way of swamping boats. In a ten-foot dinghy one can get an idea of the resources of the sea in the line of waves that is not probable to the average experience, which is never at sea in a dinghy. As each salty wall of water approached, it shut all else from the view of the men in the boat, and it was not difficult to imagine that this particular wave was the final outburst of the ocean, the last effort of the grim water. There was a terrible grace in the move of the waves, and they came in silence, save for the snarling of the crests.

In the wan light the faces of the men must have

been gray. Their eyes must have glinted in strange ways as they gazed steadily astern. Viewed from a balcony, the whole thing would, doubtless, have been weirdly picturesque. But the men in the boat had no time to see it, and if they had had leisure, there were other things to occupy their minds. The sun swung steadily up the sky, and they knew it was broad day because the color of the sea changed from slate to emerald-green streaked with amber lights, and the foam was like tumbling snow. The process of the breaking day was unknown to them. They were aware only of this effect upon the color of the waves that rolled toward them.

In disjointed sentences the cook and the correspondent argued as to the difference between a life-saving station and a house of refuge. The cook had said: "There's a house of refuge just north of the Mosquito Inlet Light, and as soon as they see us they'll come off in their boat and pick us up."

"As soon as who see us?" said the correspondent.

"The crew," said the cook.

"Houses of refuge don't have crews," said the correspondent. "As I understand them, they are only places where clothes and grub are stored for the benefit of shipwrecked people. They don't carry crews."

"Oh, yes, they do," said the cook.

"No, they don't," said the correspondent.

"Well, we're not there yet, anyhow," said the oiler in the stern.

"Well," said the cook, "perhaps it's not a house of refuge that I'm thinking of as being near Mosquito Inlet Light; perhaps it's a life-saving station."

"We're not there yet," said the oiler in the stern.

II

As the boat bounced from the top of each wave the wind tore through the hair of the hatless men, and as the craft plopped her stern down again the spray slashed past them. The crest of each of these waves was a hill, from the top of which the men surveyed for a moment a broad, tumultuous expanse, shining and wind-riven. It was probably splendid, it was probably glorious, this play of the free sea, wild with lights of emerald and white and amber.

"Bully good thing it's an on-shore wind," said the cook. "If not, where would we be? Wouldn't have a show."

"That's right," said the correspondent.

The busy oiler nodded his assent.

Then the captain, in the bow, chuckled in a way that expressed humor, contempt, tragedy, all in one. "Do you think we've got much of a show now, boys?" said he.

Whereupon the three were silent, save for a trifle of hemming and hawing. To express any particular optimism at this time they felt to be childish and stupid, but they all doubtless possessed this sense of the situation in their minds. A young man thinks doggedly at such times. On the other hand, the ethics of their condition was decidedly against any open suggestion of hopelessness. So they were silent.

"Oh, well," said the captain, soothing his children, "we'll get ashore all right."

But there was that in his tone which made them think; so the oiler quoth, "Yes! if this wind holds."

The cook was bailing. "Yes! if we don't catch hell in the surf."

Canton-flannel gulls flew near and far. Sometimes they sat down on the sea, near patches of brown seaweed that rolled over the waves with a movement like carpets on a line in a gale. The birds sat comfortably in groups, and they were envied by some in the dinghy, for the wrath of the sea was no more to them than it was to a covey of prairie-chickens a thousand miles inland. Often they came very close and stared at the men with black, bead-like eyes. At these times they were uncanny and sinister in their unblinking scrutiny, and the men hooted angrily at them, telling them to be gone. One came, and evidently decided to alight on the top of the captain's head. The bird flew parallel to the boat, and did not circle, but made short sidelong jumps in the air in chicken fashion. His black eyes were wistfully fixed upon the captain's head. "Ugly brute," said the oiler to the bird. "You look as if you were made with a jack-knife." The cook and the correspondent swore darkly at the creature. The captain naturally wished to knock it away with the end of the heavy painter, but he did not dare do it, because anything resembling an emphatic gesture would have capsized this freighted boat; and so, with his open hand, the captain gently and carefully waved the gull away. After it had been discouraged from the pursuit the captain breathed easier on account of his hair, and others breathed easier because the bird struck their minds at this time as being somehow gruesome and ominous.

In the meantime the oiler and the correspondent rowed; and also they rowed. They sat together in the same seat, and each rowed an oar. Then the oiler took both oars; then the correspondent took both oars; then the oiler; then the correspondent. They rowed and they rowed. The very ticklish part of the business was when the time came for the reclining one in the stern to take his turn at the oars. By the very last star of truth, it is easier to steal eggs from under a hen than it was to change seats in the dinghy. First the man in the stern slid his hand along the thwart and moved with care, as if he were of Sèvres. Then the man in the rowing-seat slid his hand along the other thwart. It was all done with the most extraordinary care. As the two sidled past each other, the whole party kept watchful eyes on the coming wave, and the captain cried: "Look out, now! Steady, there!"

The brown mats of seaweed that appeared from time to time were like islands, bits of earth. They were traveling, apparently, neither one way nor the other. They were, to all intents, stationary. They informed the men in the boat that it was making progress slowly toward the land.

The captain, rearing cautiously in the bow after the dinghy soared on a great swell, said that he had seen the lighthouse at Mosquito Inlet. Presently the cook remarked that he had seen it. The correspondent was at the oars then, and for some reason he too wished to look at the lighthouse; but his back was toward the far shore, and the waves were important, and for some time he could not seize an opportunity to turn his head. But at last there came a wave more gentle than the others, and when at the crest of it he swiftly scoured the western horizon.

"See it?" said the captain.

"No," said the correspondent, slowly; "I didn't see anything."

"Look again," said the captain. He pointed. "It's exactly in that direction."

At the top of another wave the correspondent did as he was bid, and this time his eyes chanced on a small, still thing on the edge of the swaying horizon. It was precisely like the point of a pin. It took an anxious eye to find a lighthouse so tiny.

"Think we'll make it, Captain?"

"If this wind holds and the boat don't swamp, we can't do much else," said the captain.

The little boat, lifted by each towering sea and splashed viciously by the crests, made progress that in the absence of seaweed was not apparent to those in her. She seemed just a wee thing wallowing miraculously, top up, at the mercy of five oceans. Occasionally a great spread of water, like white flames, swarmed into her.

"Bail her, cook," said the captain, serenely.

"All right, Captain," said the cheerful cook.

III

It would be difficult to describe the subtle brotherhood of men that was here established on the seas. No one said that it was so. No one mentioned it. But it dwelt in the boat, and each man felt it warm him.

They were a captain, an oiler, a cook, and a correspondent, and they were friends—friends in a more curiously iron-bound degree than may be common. The hurt captain, lying against the water-jar in the bow, spoke always in a low voice and calmly; but he could never command a more ready and swiftly obedient crew than the motley three of the dinghy. It was more than a mere recognition of what was best for the common safety. There was surely in it a quality that was personal and heartfelt. And after this devotion to the commander of the boat, there was this comradeship, that the correspondent, for instance, who had been taught to be cynical of men, knew even at the time was the best experience of his life. But no one said that it was so. No one mentioned it.

"I wish we had a sail," remarked the captain. "We might try my overcoat on the end of an oar, and give you two boys a chance to rest." So the cook and the correspondent held the mast and spread wide the overcoat; the oiler steered; and the little boat made good way with her new rig. Sometimes the oiler had to scull sharply to keep a sea from breaking into the boat, but otherwise sailing was a success.

Meanwhile the lighthouse had been growing slowly larger. It had now almost assumed color, and appeared like a little gray shadow on the sky. The man at the oars could not be prevented from turning his head rather often to try for a glimpse of this little gray shadow.

At last, from the top of each wave, the men in the tossing boat could see land. Even as the lighthouse was an upright shadow on the sky, this land seemed but a long black shadow on the sea. It certainly was thinner than paper. "We must be about opposite New Smyrna," said the cook, who had coasted this shore often in schooners. "Captain, by the way, I believe they abandoned that life-saving station there about a year ago."

"Did they?" said the captain.

The wind slowly died away. The cook and the correspondent were not now obliged to slave in order to hold high the oar; but the waves continued their old impetuous swooping at the dinghy, and the little craft, no longer under way, struggled woundily over them. The oiler or the correspondent took the oars again.

Shipwrecks are *apropos* of nothing. If men could only train for them and have them occur when the men had reached pink condition, there would be less drowning at sea. Of the four in the dinghy none had slept any time worth mentioning for two days and two nights previous to embarking in the dinghy, and in the excitement of clambering about the deck of a foundering ship they had also forgotten to eat heartily.

For these reasons, and for others, neither the oiler nor the correspondent was fond of rowing at this time. The correspondent wondered ingenuously how in the name of all that was sane could there be people who thought it amusing to row a boat. It was not an amusement; it was a diabolical punishment, and even a genius of mental aberrations could never conclude that it was anything but a horror to the muscles and a crime against the back. He mentioned to the boat in general how the amusement of rowing struck him, and the weary-faced oiler smiled in full sympathy. Previously to the foundering, by the way, the oiler had worked double watch in the engine-room of the ship.

"Take her easy now, boys," said the captain. "Don't spend yourselves. If we have to run a surf you'll need all your strength, because we'll sure have to swim for it. Take your time."

Slowly the land arose from the sea. From a black line it became a line of black and a line of white—trees and sand. Finally the captain said that he could make out a house on the shore. "That's the house of refuge, sure," said the cook. "They'll see us before long, and come out after us."

The distant lighthouse reared high. "The keeper

ought to be able to make us out now, if he's looking through a glass," said the captain. "He'll notify the life-saving people."

"None of those other boats could have got ashore to give word of the wreck," said the oiler, in a low voice, "else the life-boat would be out hunting us."

Slowly and beautifully the land loomed out of the sea. The wind came again. It had veered from the northeast to the southeast. Finally a new sound struck the ears of the men in the boat. It was the low thunder of the surf on the shore. "We'll never be able to make the lighthouse now," said the captain. "Swing her head a little more north, Billie."

"A little more north, sir," said the oiler.

Whereupon the little boat turned her nose once more down the wind, and all but the oarsman watched the shore grow. Under the influence of this expansion doubt and direful apprehension were leaving the minds of the men. The management of the boat was still most absorbing, but it could not prevent a quiet cheerfulness. In an hour, perhaps, they would be ashore.

Their backbones had become thoroughly used to balancing in the boat, and they now rode this wild colt of a dinghy like circus men. The correspondent thought that he had been drenched to the skin, but happening to feel in the top pocket of his coat, he found therein eight cigars. Four of them were soaked with sea-water; four were perfectly scatheless. After a search, somebody produced three dry matches; and thereupon the four waifs rode in their little boat and, with an assurance of an impending rescue shining in their eyes, puffed at the big cigars, and judged well and ill of all men. Everybody took a drink of water.

IV

"Cook," remarked the captain, "there don't seem to be any signs of life about your house of refuge."

"No," replied the cook. "Funny they don't see us!"

A broad stretch of lowly coast lay before the eyes of the men. It was of low dunes topped with dark vegetation. The roar of the surf was plain, and sometimes they could see the white lip of a wave as it spun up the beach. A tiny house was blocked out black upon the sky. Southward, the slim lighthouse lifted its little gray length.

Tide, wind, and waves were swinging the dinghy northward. "Funny they don't see us," said the men.

The surf's roar was here dulled, but its tone was nevertheless thunderous and mighty. As the boat swam over the great rollers the men sat listening to this roar. "We'll swamp sure," said everybody.

It is fair to say here that there was not a life-saving station within twenty miles in either direction;

but the men did not know this fact, and in consequence they made dark and opprobrious remarks concerning the eyesight of the nation's life-savers. Four scowling men sat in the dinghy, and surpassed records in the invention of epithets.

"Funny they don't see us."

The light-heartedness of a former time had completely faded. To their sharpened minds it was easy to conjure pictures of all kinds of incompetency and blindness and, indeed, cowardice. There was the shore of the populous land, and it was bitter and bitter to them that from it came no sign.

"Well," said the captain, ultimately, "I suppose we'll have to make a try for ourselves. If we stay out here too long, we'll none of us have strength left to swim after the boat swamps."

And so the oiler, who was at the oars, turned the boat straight for the shore. There was a sudden tightening of muscles. There was some thinking.

"If we don't all get ashore," said the captain, "if we don't all get ashore, I suppose you fellows know where to send news of my finish?"

They then briefly exchanged some addresses and admonitions. As for the reflections of the men, there was a great deal of rage in them. Perchance they might be formulated thus: "If I am going to be drowned—if I am going to be drowned—if I am going to be drowned, why, in the name of the seven mad gods who rule the sea, was I allowed to come thus far and contemplate sand and trees? Was I brought here merely to have my nose dragged away as I was about to nibble the sacred cheese of life? It is preposterous! If this old ninny-woman, Fate, cannot do better than this, she should be deprived of the management of men's fortunes. She is an old hen who knows not her intention. If she has decided to drown me, why did she not do it in the beginning, and save me all this trouble? The whole affair is absurd . . . But no; she cannot mean to drown me. She dare not drown me. She cannot drown me. Not after all this work!" Afterward the man might have had an impulse to shake his fist at the clouds. "Just you drown me, now, and then hear what I call you!"

The billows that came at this time were more formidable. They seemed always just about to break and roll over the little boat in a turmoil of foam. There was a preparatory and long growl in the speech of them. No mind unused to the sea would have concluded that the dinghy could ascend these sheer heights in time. The shore was still afar. The oiler was a wily surfman. "Boys," he said swiftly, "she won't live three minutes more, and we're too far out to swim. Shall I take her to sea again, Captain?"

"Yes; go ahead!" said the captain.

This oiler, by a series of quick miracles and fast and steady oarsmanship, turned the boat in the middle of the surf and took her safely to sea again.

There was a considerable silence as the boat bumped over the furrowed sea to deeper water. Then somebody in gloom spoke: "Well, anyhow, they must have seen us from the shore by now."

The gulls went in slanting flight up the wind toward the gray, desolate east. A squall, marked by dingy clouds, and clouds brick-red, like smoke from a burning building, appeared from the southeast.

"What do you think of those life-saving people? Ain't they peaches?"

"Funny they haven't seen us."

"Maybe they think we're out here for sport! Maybe they think we're fishin'. Maybe they think we're damned fools."

It was a long afternoon. A changed tide tried to force them southward, but wind and wave said northward. Far ahead, where coast-line, sea, and sky formed their mighty angle, there were little dots which seemed to indicate a city on the shore.

"St. Augustine?"

The captain shook his head. "Too near Mosquito Inlet."

And the oiler rowed, and then the correspondent

rowed; then the oiler rowed. It was a weary business. The human back can become the seat of more aches and pains than are registered in books for the composite anatomy of a regiment. It is a limited area, but it can become the theater of innumerable muscular conflicts, tangles, wrenches, knots, and other comforts.

"Did you ever like to row, Billie?" asked the correspondent.

"No," said the oiler; "hang it!"

When one exchanged the rowing-seat for a place in the bottom of the boat, he suffered a bodily depression that caused him to be careless of everything save an obligation to wiggle one finger. There was cold sea-water swashing to and fro in the boat, and he lay in it. His head, pillowed on a thwart, was within an inch of the swirl of a wave-crest, and sometimes a particularly obstreperous sea came inboard and drenched him once more. But these matters did not annoy him. It is almost certain that if the boat had capsized he would have tumbled comfortably out upon the ocean as if he felt sure that it was a great, soft mattress.

"Look! There's a man on the shore!"

"Where?"

"There! See 'im? See 'im?"

"Yes, sure! He's walking along."

"Now he's stopped. Look! He's facing us!"

"He's waving at us!"

"So he is! By thunder!"

"Ah, now we're all right! Now we're all right! There'll be a boat out here for us in half an hour."

"He's going on. He's running. He's going up to that house there."

The remote beach seemed lower than the sea, and it required a searching glance to discern the little black figure. The captain saw a floating stick, and they rowed to it. A bath towel was by some weird chance in the boat, and tying this on the stick, the captain waved it. The oarsman did not dare turn his head, so he was obliged to ask questions.

"What's he doing now?"

"He's standing still again. He's looking, I think . . . There he goes again—toward the house . . . Now he's stopped again."

"Is he waving at us?"

"No, not now; he was, though."

"Look! There comes another man!"

"He's running."

"Look at him go, would you!"

"Why, he's on a bicycle. Now he's met the other man. They're both waving at us. Look!"

"There comes something up the beach."

"What the devil is that thing?"

"Why, it looks like a boat."

"Why, certainly, it's a boat."

"No; it's on wheels."

"Yes, so it is. Well, that must be the life-boat. They drag them along shore on a wagon."

"That's the life-boat, sure."

"No, by——, it's—it's an omnibus."

"I tell you it's a life-boat."

"It is not! It's an omnibus. I can see it plain. See? One of these big hotel omnibuses."

"By thunder, you're right. It's an omnibus, sure as fate. What do you suppose they are doing with an omnibus? Maybe they are going around collecting the life-crew, hey?"

"That's it, likely. Look! There's a fellow waving a little black flag. He's standing on the steps of the omnibus. There come those other two fellows. Now they're all talking together. Look at the fellow with the flag. Maybe he ain't waving it!"

"That ain't a flag, is it? That's his coat. Why, certainly, that's his coat."

"So it is; it's his coat. He's taken it off and is waving it around his head. But would you look at him swing it!"

"Oh, say, there isn't any life-saving station there. That's just a winter-resort hotel omnibus that has brought over some of the boarders to see us drown."

"What's that idiot with the coat mean? What's he signaling, anyhow?"

"It looks as if he were trying to tell us to go north. There must be a life-saving station up there."

"No; he thinks we're fishing. Just giving us a merry hand. See? Ah, there, Willie!"

"Well, I wish I could make something out of those signals. What do you suppose he means?"

"He don't mean anything; he's just playing."

"Well, if he'd just signal us to try the surf again, or to go to sea and wait, or go north, or go south, or go to hell, there would be some reason in it. But look at him! He just stands there and keeps his coat revolving like a wheel. The ass!"

"There come more people."

"Now there's quite a mob. Look! Isn't that a boat?"

"Where? Oh, I see where you mean. No, that's no boat."

"That fellow is still waving his coat."

"He must think we like to see him do that. Why don't he quit it? It don't mean anything."

"I don't know. I think he is trying to make us go north. It must be that there's a life-saving station there some-where."

"Say, he ain't tired yet. Look at 'im wave!"

"Wonder how long he can keep that up. He's

been revolving his coat ever since he caught sight of us. He's an idiot. Why aren't they getting men to bring a boat out? A fishing-boat—one of those big yawls—could come out here all right. Why don't he do something?"

"Oh, it's all right now."

"They'll have a boat out here for us in less than no time, now that they've seen us."

A faint yellow tone came into the sky over the low land. The shadows on the sea slowly deepened. The wind bore coldness with it, and the men began to shiver.

"Holy smoke!" said one, allowing his voice to express his impious mood, "if we keep on monkeying out here! If we've got to flounder out here all night!"

"Oh, we'll never have to stay here all night! Don't you worry. They've seen us now, and it won't be long before they'll come chasing out after us."

The shore grew dusky. The man waving a coat blended gradually into this gloom, and it swallowed in the same manner the omnibus and the group of people. The spray, when it dashed uproariously over the side, made the voyagers shrink and swear like men who were being branded.

"I'd like to catch the chump who waved the coat. I feel like soaking him one, just for luck."

"Why? What did he do?"

"Oh, nothing, but then he seemed so damned cheerful."

In the meantime the oiler rowed, and then the correspondent rowed, and then the oiler rowed. Gray-faced and bowed forward, they mechanically, turn by turn, plied the leaden oars. The form of the lighthouse had vanished from the southern horizon, but finally a pale star appeared, just lifting from the sea. The streaked saffron in the west passed before the all-merging darkness, and the sea to the east was black. The land had vanished, and was expressed only by the low and drear thunder of the surf.

"If I am going to be drowned—if I am going to be drowned—if I am going to be drowned, why, in the name of the seven mad gods who rule the sea, was I allowed to come thus far and contemplate sand and trees? Was I brought here merely to have my nose dragged away as I was about to nibble the sacred cheese of life?"

The patient captain, drooped over the water-jar, was sometimes obliged to speak to the oarsman.

"Keep her head up! Keep her head up!"

"Keep her head up, sir." The voices were weary and low.

This was surely a quiet evening. All save the oarsman lay heavily and listlessly in the boat's bottom. As for him, his eyes were just capable of noting the tall black waves that swept forward in a most sinister silence, save for an occasional subdued growl of a crest.

The cook's head was on a thwart, and he looked without interest at the water under his nose. He was deep in other scenes. Finally he spoke. "Billie," he murmured dreamfully, "what kind of pie do you like best?"

V

"Pie!" said the oiler and the correspondent, agitatedly. "Don't talk about those things, blast you!"

"Well," said the cook, "I was just thinking about ham sandwiches, and—"

A night on the sea in an open boat is a long night. As darkness settled finally, the shine of the light, lifting from the sea in the south, changed to full gold. On the northern horizon a new light appeared, a small bluish gleam on the edge of the waters. These two lights were the furniture of the world. Otherwise there was nothing but waves.

Two men huddled in the stern, and distances were so magnificent in the dinghy that the rower was enabled to keep his feet partly warm by thrusting them under his companions. Their legs indeed extended far under the rowing-seat until they touched the feet of the captain forward. Sometimes, despite the efforts of the tired oarsman, a wave came piling into the boat, an icy wave of the night, and the chilling water soaked them anew. They would twist their bodies for a moment and groan, and sleep the dead sleep once more, while the water in the boat gurgled about them as the craft rocked.

The plan of the oiler and the correspondent was for one to row until he lost the ability, and then arouse the other from his sea-water couch in the bottom of the boat.

The oiler plied the oars until his head drooped forward and the overpowering sleep blinded him; and he rowed yet afterward. Then he touched a man in the bottom of the boat, and called his name. "Will you spell me for a little while?" he said meekly.

"Sure, Billie," said the correspondent, awaking and dragging himself to a sitting position. They exchanged places carefully, and the oiler, cuddling down in the sea-water at the cook's side, seemed to go to sleep instantly.

The particular violence of the sea had ceased. The waves came without snarling. The obligation of the man at the oars was to keep the boat headed so that the tilt of the rollers would not capsize her, and to preserve her from filling when the crests rushed past. The black waves were silent and hard to be seen in the darkness. Often one was almost upon the boat before the oarsman was aware.

In a low voice the correspondent addressed the captain. He was not sure that the captain was awake, although this iron man seemed to be always awake. "Captain, shall I keep her making for that light north, sir?"

The same steady voice answered him. "Yes. Keep it about two points off the port bow."

The cook had tied a life-belt around himself in order to get even the warmth which this clumsy cork contrivance could donate, and he seemed almost stove-like when a rower, whose teeth invariably chattered wildly as soon as he ceased his labor, dropped down to sleep.

The correspondent, as he rowed, looked down at the two men sleeping under foot. The cook's arm was around the oiler's shoulders, and, with their fragmentary clothing and haggard faces, they were the babes of the sea—a grotesque rendering of the old babes in the wood.

Later he must have grown stupid at his work, for suddenly there was a growling of water, and a crest came with a roar and a swash into the boat, and it was a wonder that it did not set the cook afloat in his life-belt. The cook continued to sleep, but the oiler sat up, blinking his eyes and shaking with the new cold.

"Oh, I'm awful sorry, Billie," said the correspondent, contritely.

"That's all right, old boy," said the oiler, and lay down again and was asleep.

Presently it seemed that even the captain dozed, and the correspondent thought that he was the one man afloat on all the oceans. The wind had a voice as it came over the waves, and it was sadder than the end.

There was a long, loud swishing astern of the boat, and a gleaming trail of phosphorescence, like blue flame, was furrowed on the black waters. It might have been made by a monstrous knife.

Then there came a stillness, while the correspondent breathed with the open mouth and looked at the sea.

Suddenly there was another swish and another long flash of bluish light, and this time it was alongside the boat, and might almost have been reached with an oar. The correspondent saw an enormous fin speed like a shadow through the water, hurling the crystalline spray and leaving the long glowing trail.

The correspondent looked over his shoulder at the captain. His face was hidden, and he seemed to be asleep. He looked at the babes of the sea. They certainly were asleep. So, being bereft of sympathy, he leaned a little way to one side and swore softly into the sea.

But the thing did not then leave the vicinity of the boat. Ahead or astern, on one side or the other, at intervals long or short, fled the long sparkling streak, and there was to be heard the whiroo of the dark fin. The speed and power of the thing was greatly to be admired. It cut the water like a gigantic and keen projectile.

The presence of this biding thing did not affect the man with the same horror that it would if he had been a picnicker. He simply looked at the sea dully and swore in an undertone.

Nevertheless, it is true that he did not wish to be alone with the thing. He wished one of his companions to awake by chance and keep him company with it. But the captain hung motionless over the water-jar, and the oiler and the cook in the bottom of the boat were plunged in slumber.

VI

"If I am going to be drowned—if I am going to be drowned—if I am going to be drowned, why, in the name of the seven mad gods who rule the sea, was I allowed to come thus far and contemplate sand and trees?"

During this dismal night, it may be remarked that a man would conclude that it was really the intention of the seven mad gods to drown him, despite the abominable injustice of it. For it was certainly an abominable injustice to drown a man who had worked so hard, so hard. The man felt it would be a crime most unnatural. Other people had drowned at sea since galleys swarmed with painted sails, but still—

When it occurs to a man that nature does not regard him as important, and that she feels she would not maim the universe by disposing of him, he at first wishes to throw bricks at the temple, and he hates deeply the fact that there are no bricks and no temples. Any visible expression of nature would surely be pelleted with his jeers.

Then, if there be no tangible thing to hoot, he feels, perhaps, the desire to confront a personification and indulge in pleas, bowed to one knee, and with hands supplicant, saying, "Yes, but I love myself."

A high cold star on a winter's night is the word he feels that she says to him. Thereafter he knows the pathos of his situation.

The men in .the dinghy had not discussed these matters, but each had, no doubt, reflected upon them in silence and according to his mind. There was seldom any expression upon their faces save the general one of complete weariness. Speech was devoted to the business of the boat.

To chime the notes of his emotion, a verse mysteriously entered the correspondent's head. He had even forgotten that he had forgotten this verse, but it suddenly was in his mind.

A soldier of the Legion lay dying in Algiers;
There was lack of woman's nursing, there was
    dearth of woman's tears;
But a comrade stood beside him, and he took
    that comrade's hand,
And he said, "I never more shall see my own,
    my native land."

In his childhood the correspondent had been made acquainted with the fact that a soldier of the Legion lay dying in Algiers, but he had never regarded it as important. Myriads of his schoolfellows had informed him of the soldier's plight, but the dinning had naturally ended by making him perfectly indifferent. He had never considered it his affair that a soldier of the Legion lay dying in Algiers, nor had it appeared to him as a matter for sorrow. It was less to him than breaking of a pencil's point.

Now, however, it quaintly came to him as a human, living thing. It was no longer merely a picture of a few throes in the breast of a poet, meanwhile drinking tea and warming his feet at the grate; it was an actuality—stern, mournful, and fine.

The correspondent plainly saw the soldier. He lay on the sand with his feet out straight and still. While his pale left hand was upon his chest in an attempt to thwart the going of his life, the blood came between his fingers. In the far Algerian distance, a city of low square forms was set against a sky that was faint with the last sunset hues. The correspondent, plying the oars and dreaming of the slow and slower movements of the lips of the soldier, was moved by a profound and perfectly impersonal comprehension. He was sorry for the soldier of the Legion who lay dying in Algiers.

The thing which had followed the boat and waited had evidently grown bored at the delay. There was no longer to be heard the slash of the cutwater, and there was no longer the flame of the long trail. The light in the north still glimmered, but it was apparently no nearer to the boat. Sometimes the boom of the surf rang in the correspondent's ears, and he turned the craft seaward then and rowed harder. Southward, some one had evidently built a watch-fire on the beach. It was too low and too far to be seen, but it made a shimmering, roseate reflection upon the bluff back of it, and this could be discerned from the boat. The wind came stronger, and sometimes a wave suddenly raged out like a mountain-cat, and there was to be seen the sheen and sparkle of a broken crest.

The captain, in the bow, moved on his water-jar and sat erect. "Pretty long night," he observed to the correspondent. He looked at the shore. "Those life-saving people take their time."

"Did you see that shark playing around?"

"Yes, I saw him. He was a big fellow, all right."

"Wish I had known you were awake."

Later the correspondent spoke into the bottom of the boat.

"Billie!" There was a slow and gradual disentanglement. "Billie, will you spell me?"

"Sure," said the oiler.

As soon as the correspondent touched the cold, comfortable sea-water in the bottom of the boat and had huddled close to the cook's life-belt he was deep in sleep, despite the fact that his teeth played all the popular airs. This sleep was so good to him that it was but a moment before he heard a voice call his name in a tone that demonstrated the last stages of exhaustion. "Will you spell me?"

"Sure, Billie."

The light in the north had mysteriously vanished, but the correspondent took his course from the wide-awake captain.

Later in the night they took the boat farther out to sea, and the captain directed the cook to take one oar at the stern and keep the boat facing the seas. He was to call out if he should hear the thunder of the surf. This plan enabled the oiler and the correspondent to get respite together. "We'll give those boys a chance to get into shape again," said the captain. They curled down and, after a few preliminary chatterings and trembles, slept once more the dead sleep. Neither knew they had bequeathed to the cook the company of another shark, or perhaps the same shark.

As the boat caroused on the waves, spray occasionally bumped over the side and gave them a fresh soaking, but this had no power to break their repose. The ominous slash of the wind and the water affected them as it would have affected mummies.

"Boys," said the cook, with the notes of every reluctance in his voice, "she's drifted in pretty close. I guess one of you had better take her to sea again."

The correspondent, aroused, heard the crash of the toppled crests.

As he was rowing, the captain gave him some whisky and water, and this steadied the chills out of him. "If I ever get ashore and anybody shows me even a photograph of an oar—"

At last there was a short conversation.

"Billie! . . . Billie, will you spell me?"

"Sure," said the oiler.

VII

When the correspondent again opened his eyes, the sea and the sky were each of the gray hue of the dawning. Later, carmine and gold was painted upon the waters. The morning appeared finally, in its splendor, with a sky of pure blue, and the sunlight flamed on the tips of the waves.

On the distant dunes were set many little black cottages, and a tall white windmill reared above them. No man, nor dog, nor bicycle appeared on the beach. The cottages might have formed a deserted village.

The voyagers scanned the shore. A conference was held in the boat. "Well," said the captain, "if no help is coming, we might better try a run through the surf right away. If we stay out here much longer we will be too weak to do anything for ourselves at all." The others silently acquiesced in this reasoning. The boat was headed for the beach. The correspondent wondered if none ever ascended the tall wind-tower, and if then they never looked seaward. This tower was a giant, standing with its back to the plight of the ants. It represented in a degree, to the correspondent, the serenity of nature amid the struggles of the individual—nature in the wind, and nature in the vision of men. She did not seem cruel to him then, nor beneficent, nor treacherous, nor wise. But she was indifferent, flatly indifferent. It is, perhaps, plausible that a man in this situation, impressed with the unconcern of the universe, should see the innumerable flaws of his life and have them taste wickedly in his mind and wish for another chance. A distinction between right and wrong seems absurdly clear to him, then, in this new ignorance of the grave-edge, and he understands that if he were given another opportunity he would mend his conduct and his words, and be better and brighter during an introduction or at a tea.

"Now, boys," said the captain, "she is going to swamp sure. All we can do is to work her in as far as possible, and then when she swamps, pile out and scramble for the beach. Keep cool now, and don't jump until she swamps sure."

The oiler took the oars. Over his shoulders he

scanned the surf. "Captain," he said, "I think I'd better bring her about, and keep her head-on to the seas, and back her in."

"All right, Billie," said the captain. "Back her in." The oiler swung the boat then, and, seated in the stern, the cook and the correspondent were obliged to look over their shoulders to contemplate the lonely and indifferent shore.

The monstrous inshore rollers heaved the boat high until the men were again enabled to see the white sheets of water scudding up the slanted beach. "We won't get in very close," said the captain. Each time a man could wrest his attention from the rollers, he turned his glance toward the shore, and in the expression of the eyes during this contemplation there was a singular quality. The correspondent, observing the others, knew that they were not afraid, but the full meaning of their glances was shrouded.

As for himself, he was too tired to grapple fundamentally with the fact. He tried to coerce his mind into thinking of it, but the mind was dominated at this time by the muscles, and the muscles said they did not care. It merely occurred to him that if he should drown it would be a shame.

There were no hurried words, no pallor, no plain agitation. The men simply looked at the shore.

"Now, remember to get well clear of the boat when you jump," said the captain.

Seaward the crest of a roller suddenly fell with a thunderous crash, and the long white comber came roaring down upon the boat.

"Steady now," said the captain. The men were silent. They turned their eyes from the shore to the comber and waited. The boat slid up the incline, leaped at the furious top, bounced over it, and swung down the long back of the wave. Some water had been shipped, and the cook bailed it out.

But the next crest crashed also. The tumbling, boiling flood of white water caught the boat and whirled it almost perpendicular. Water swarmed in from all sides. The correspondent had his hands on the gunwale at this time, and when the water entered at that place he swiftly withdrew his fingers, as if he objected to wetting them.

The little boat, drunken with this weight of water, reeled and snuggled deeper into the sea.

"Bail her out, cook! Bail her out!" said the captain.

"All right, Captain," said the cook.

"Now, boys, the next one will do for us sure," said the oiler. "Mind to jump clear of the boat."

The third wave moved forward, huge, furious, implacable. It fairly swallowed the dinghy, and almost simultaneously the men tumbled into the sea. A piece of life-belt had lain in the bottom of the boat, and as the correspondent went overboard he held this to his chest with his left hand.

The January water was icy, and he reflected immediately that it was colder than he had expected to find it off the coast of Florida. This appeared to his dazed mind as a fact important enough to be noted at the time. The coldness of the water was sad; it was tragic. This fact was somehow mixed and confused with his opinion of his own situation so that it seemed almost a proper reason for tears. The water was cold.

When he came to the surface he was conscious of little but the noisy water. Afterward he saw his companions in the sea. The oiler was ahead in the race. He was swimming strongly and rapidly. Off to the correspondent's left, the cook's great white and corked back bulged out of the water; and in the rear the captain was hanging with his one good hand to the keel of the overturned dinghy.

There is a certain immovable quality to a shore, and the correspondent wondered at it amid the confusion of the sea.

It seemed also very attractive; but the correspondent knew that it was a long journey, and he paddled leisurely. The piece of life-preserver lay under him, and sometimes he whirled down the incline of a wave as if he were on a hand-sled.

But finally he arrived at a place in the sea where travel was beset with difficulty. He did not pause swimming to inquire what manner of current had caught him, but there his progress ceased. The shore was set before him like a bit of scenery on a stage, and he looked at it, and understood with his eyes each detail of it.

As the cook passed, much farther to the left, the captain was calling to him, "Turn over on your back, cook! Turn over on your back and use the oar."

"All right, sir." The cook turned on his back, and, paddling with an oar, went ahead as if he were a canoe.

Presently the boat also passed to the left of the correspondent, with the captain clinging with one hand to the keel. He would have appeared like a man raising himself to look over a board fence if it were not for the extraordinary gymnastics of the boat. The correspondent marveled that the captain could still hold to it.

They passed on nearer to shore,—the oiler, the cook, the captain,—and following them went the water-jar, bouncing gaily over the seas.

The correspondent remained in the grip of this strange new enemy, a current. The shore, with its white slope of sand and its green bluff, topped with little silent cottages, was spread like a picture before him. It was very near to him then, but he was impressed as one who, in a gallery, looks at a scene from Brittany or Algiers.

He thought: "I am going to drown? Can it be possible? Can it be possible? Can it be possible?" Perhaps an individual must consider his own death to be the final phenomenon of nature.

But later a wave perhaps whirled him out of this small deadly current, for he found suddenly that he could again make progress toward the shore. Later still he was aware that the captain, clinging with one hand to the keel of the dinghy, had his face turned away from the shore and toward him, and was calling his name. "Come to the boat! Come to the boat!"

In his struggle to reach the captain and the boat, he reflected that when one gets properly wearied drowning must really be a comfortable arrangement—a cessation of hostilities accompanied by a large degree of relief; and he was glad of it, for the main thing in his mind for some moments had been horror of the temporary agony; he did not wish to be hurt.

Presently he saw a man running along the shore. He was undressing with most remarkable speed.

Coat, trousers, shirt, everything flew magically off him.

"Come to the boat!" called the captain.

"All right, Captain." As the correspondent paddled, he saw the captain let himself down to bottom and leave the boat. Then the correspondent performed his one little marvel of the voyage. A large wave caught him and flung him with ease and supreme speed completely over the boat and far beyond it. It struck him even then as an event in gymnastics and a true miracle of the sea. An overturned boat in the surf is not a plaything to a swimming man.

The correspondent arrived in water that reached only to his waist, but his condition did not enable him to stand for more than a moment. Each wave knocked him into a heap, and the undertow pulled at him.

Then he saw the man who had been running and undressing, and undressing and running, come bounding into the water. He dragged ashore the cook, and then waded toward the captain; but the captain waved him away and sent him to the correspondent. He was naked—naked as a tree in winter; but a halo was about his head, and he shone like a saint. He gave a strong pull, and a long drag, and a bully heave at the correspondent's hand. The correspondent, schooled in the minor formulæ, said, "Thanks, old man." But suddenly the man cried, "What's that?" He pointed a swift finger. The correspondent said, "Go."

In the shallows, face downward, lay the oiler. His forehead touched sand that was periodically, between each wave, clear of the sea.

The correspondent did not know all that transpired afterward. When he achieved safe ground he fell, striking the sand with each particular part of his body. It was as if he had dropped from a roof, but the thud was grateful to him.

It seems that instantly the beach was populated with men with blankets, clothes, and flasks, and women with coffee-pots and all the remedies sacred to their minds. The welcome of the land to the men from the sea was warm and generous; but a still and dripping shape was carried slowly up the beach, and the land's welcome for it could only be the different and sinister hospitality of the grave.

When it came night, the white waves paced to and fro in the moonlight, and the wind brought the sound of the great sea's voice to the men on shore, and they felt that they could then be interpreters.

JOSEPH CONRAD

The Secret Sharer

I

On my right hand there were lines of fishing-stakes resembling a mysterious system of half-submerged bamboo fences, incomprehensible in its division of the domain of tropical fishes, and crazy of aspect as if abandoned for ever by some nomad tribe of fishermen now gone to the other end of the ocean; for there was no sign of human habitation as far as the eye could reach. To the left a group of barren islets, suggesting ruins of stone walls, towers, and block-houses, had its foundations set in a blue sea that itself looked solid, so still and stable did it lie below my feet; even the track of light from the westering sun shone smoothly, without that animated glitter which tells of an imperceptible ripple. And when I turned my head to take a parting glance at the tug which had just left us anchored outside the bar, I saw the straight line of the flat shore joined to the stable sea, edge to edge, with a perfect and unmarked closeness, in one levelled floor half brown, half blue under the enormous dome of the sky. Corresponding in their insignificance to the islets of the sea, two small clumps of trees, one on each side of the only fault in the impeccable joint, marked the mouth of the river Meinam we had just left on the first preparatory stage of our homeward journey; and, far back on the inland level, a larger and loftier mass, the grove surrounding the great Paknam pagoda, was the only thing on which the eye could rest from the vain task of exploring the monotonous sweep of the horizon. Here and there gleams as of a few scattered pieces of silver marked the windings of the great river; and on the nearest of them, just within the bar, the tug steaming right into the land became lost to my sight, hull and funnel and masts, as though the impassive earth had swallowed her up without an effort, without a tremor. My eye followed the light cloud of her smoke, now here, now there, above the plain, according to the devious curves of the stream, but always fainter and further away, till I lost it at last behind the mitre-shaped hill of the great pagoda. And then I was left alone with my ship, anchored at the head of the Gulf of Siam.

She floated at the starting-point of a long journey, very still in an immense stillness, the shadows of her spars flung far to the eastward by the setting sun. At that moment I was alone on her decks. There was not a sound in her—and around us nothing moved, nothing lived, not a canoe on the water, not a bird in the air, not a cloud in the sky. In this breathless pause at the threshold of a long passage we seemed to be measuring our fitness for a long and arduous enterprise, the appointed task of both our existences to be carried out, far from all human eyes, with only sky and sea for spectators and for judges.

There must have been some glare in the air to interfere with one's sight, because it was only just before the sun left us that my roaming eyes made out beyond the highest ridge of the principal islet of the group something which did away with the solemnity of perfect solitude. The tide of darkness flowed on swiftly; and with tropical suddenness a swarm of stars came out above the shadowy earth, while I lingered yet, my hand resting lightly on my ship's rail as if on the shoulder of a trusted friend. But, with all that multitude of celestial bodies staring down at one, the comfort of quiet communion with her was gone for good. And there were also disturbing sounds by this time—voices, footsteps forward; the steward flitted along the main-deck, a busily ministering spirit; a hand-bell tinkled urgently under the poop-deck . . .

I found my two officers waiting for me near the

supper table, in the lighted cuddy. We sat down at once, and as I helped the chief mate, I said:

'Are you aware that there is a ship anchored inside the islands? I saw her mastheads above the ridge as the sun went down.'

He raised sharply his simple face, overcharged by a terrible growth of whisker, and emitted his usual ejaculations: 'Bless my soul, sir! You don't say so!'

My second mate was a round-cheeked, silent young man, grave beyond his years, I thought; but as our eyes happened to meet I detected a slight quiver on his lips. I looked down at once. It was not my part to encourage sneering on board my ship. It must be said, too, that I knew very little of my officers. In consequence of certain events of no particular significance, except to myself, I had been appointed to the command only a fortnight before. Neither did I know much of the hands forward. All these people had been together for eighteen months or so, and my position was that of the only stranger on board. I mention this because it has some bearing on what is to follow. But what I felt most was my being a stranger to the ship; and if all the truth must be told, I was somewhat of a stranger to myself. The youngest man on board (barring the second mate), and untried as yet by a position of the fullest responsibility, I was willing to take the adequacy of the others for granted. They had simply to be equal to their tasks; but I wondered how far I should turn out faithful to that ideal conception of one's own personality every man sets up for himself secretly.

Meantime the chief mate, with an almost visible effect of collaboration on the part of his round eyes and frightful whiskers, was trying to evolve a theory of the anchored ship. His dominant trait was to take all things into earnest consideration. He was of a painstaking turn of mind. As he used to say, he 'liked to account to himself' for practically everything that came in his way, down to a miserable scorpion he had found in his cabin a week before. The why and the wherefore of that scorpion—how it got on board and came to select his room rather than the pantry (which was a dark place and more what a scorpion would be partial to), and how on earth it managed to drown itself in the inkwell of his writing-desk—had exercised him infinitely. The ship within the islands was much more easily accounted for; and just as we were about to rise from table he made his pronouncement. She was, he doubted not, a ship from home lately arrived. Probably she drew too much water to cross the bar except at the top of spring tides. Therefore she went into that natural harbour to wait for a few days in preference to remaining in an open roadstead.

'That's so,' confirmed the second mate, suddenly, in his slightly hoarse voice. 'She draws over twenty feet. She's the Liverpool ship *Sephora* with a cargo of coal. Hundred and twenty-three days from Cardiff.'

We looked at him in surprise.

'The tugboat skipper told me when he came on board for your letters, sir,' explained the young man. 'He expects to take her up the river the day after tomorrow.'

After thus overwhelming us with the extent of his information he slipped out of the cabin. The mate observed regretfully that he 'could not account for that young fellow's whims'. What prevented him telling us all about it at once, he wanted to know.

I detained him as he was making a move. For the last two days the crew had had plenty of hard work, and the night before they had very little sleep. I felt painfully that I—a stranger—was doing something unusual when I directed him to let all hands turn in without setting an anchor-watch. I proposed to keep on deck myself till one o'clock or thereabouts. I would get the second mate to relieve me at that hour.

'He will turn out the cook and the steward at four', I concluded, 'and then give you a call. Of course at the slightest sign of any sort of wind we'll have the hands up and make a start at once.'

He concealed his astonishment. 'Very well, sir.' Outside the cuddy he put his head in the second mate's door to inform him of my unheard-of caprice to take a five hours' anchor-watch on myself. I heard the other raise his voice incredulously—'What? The Captain himself?' Then a few more murmurs, a door closed, then another. A few moments later I went on deck.

My strangeness, which had made me sleepless, had prompted that unconventional arrangement, as if I had expected in those solitary hours of the night to get on terms with the ship of which I knew nothing, manned by men of whom I knew very little more. Fast alongside a wharf, littered like any ship in port with a tangle of unrelated things, invaded by unrelated shore people, I had hardly seen her yet properly. Now, as she lay cleared for sea, the stretch of her main-deck seemed to me very fine under the stars. Very fine, very roomy for her size, and very inviting. I descended the poop and paced the waist, my mind picturing to myself the coming passage through the Malay Archipelago, down the Indian Ocean, and up the Atlantic. All its phases were familiar enough to me, every characteristic, all the alternatives which were likely to face me on the high seas—everything! . . . except the novel responsibility of command. But I took heart from the reasonable thought that the ship was like other ships, the men like other men, and that the sea was not likely to keep any special surprises expressly for my discomfiture.

Arrived at that comforting conclusion, I bethought myself of a cigar and went below to get it. All was still down there. Everybody at the after end of the ship was sleeping profoundly. I came out again on the quarter-deck, agreeably at ease in my sleeping-suit on that warm breathless night, barefooted, a glowing cigar in my teeth, and, going forward, I was met by the profound silence of the fore end of the ship. Only as I passed the door of the forecastle I heard a deep, quiet, trustful sigh of some sleeper inside. And suddenly I rejoiced in the great security of the sea as compared with the unrest of the land, in my choice of that untempted life presenting no disquieting problems, invested with an elementary moral beauty by the absolute straightforwardness of its appeal and by the singleness of its purpose.

The riding-light in the fore-rigging burned with a clear, un-troubled, as if symbolic, flame, confident and bright in the mysterious shades of the night. Passing on my way aft along the other side of the ship, I observed that the rope side-ladder, put over, no doubt, for the master of the tug when he came to fetch away our letters, had not been hauled in as it should have been. I became annoyed at this, for exactitude in small matters is the very soul of discipline. Then I reflected that I had myself peremptorily dismissed my officers from duty, and by my own act had prevented the anchor-watch being formally set and things properly attended to. I asked myself whether it was wise ever to interfere with the established routine of duties even from the kindest of motives. My action might have made me appear eccentric. Goodness only knew how that absurdly whiskered mate would 'account' for my conduct, and what the whole ship thought of that informality of their new captain. I was vexed with myself.

Not from compunction certainly, but, as it were mechanically, I proceeded to get the ladder in myself. Now a side-ladder of that sort is a light affair and comes in easily, yet my vigorous tug, which should have brought it flying on board, merely recoiled upon my body in a totally unexpected jerk. What the devil! . . . I was so astounded by the immovableness of that ladder that I remained stock-still, trying to account for it to myself like that imbecile mate of mine. In the end, of course, I put my head over the rail.

The side of the ship made an opaque belt of shadow on the darkling glassy shimmer of the sea. But I saw at once something elongated and pale floating very close to the ladder. Before I could form a guess a faint flash of phosphorescent light, which seemed to issue suddenly from the naked body of a man, flickered in the sleeping water with the elusive, silent play of summer lightning in a night sky. With a gasp I saw revealed to my stare a pair of feet, the long legs, a broad livid back immersed right up to the neck in a greenish cadaverous glow. One hand, awash, clutched the bottom rung of the ladder. He was complete but for the head. A headless corpse! The cigar dropped out of my gaping mouth with a tiny plop and a short hiss quite audible in the absolute stillness of all things under heaven. At that I suppose he raised up his face, a dimly pale oval in the shadow of the ship's side. But even then I could only barely make out down there the shape of his black-haired head. However, it was enough for the horrid, frost-bound sensation which had gripped me about the chest to pass off. The moment of vain exclamations was past, too. I only climbed on the spare spar and leaned over the rail as far as I could, to bring my eyes nearer to that mystery floating alongside.

As he hung by the ladder, like a resting swimmer,

the sea-lightning played about his limbs at every stir; and he appeared in it ghastly, silvery, fish-like. He remained as mute as a fish, too. He made no motion to get out of the water, either. It was inconceivable that he should not attempt to come on board, and strangely troubling to suspect that perhaps he did not want to. And my first words were prompted by just that troubled incertitude.

'What's the matter?' I asked in my ordinary tone, speaking down to the face upturned exactly under mine.

'Cramp,' it answered, no louder. Then slightly anxious, 'I say, no need to call anyone.'

'I was not going to,' I said.

'Are you alone on deck?'

'Yes.'

I had somehow the impression that he was on the point of letting go the ladder to swim away beyond my ken—mysterious as he came. But, for the moment, this being appearing as if he had risen from the bottom of the sea (it was certainly the nearest land to the ship) wanted only to know the time. I told him. And he, down there, tentatively:

'I suppose your captain's turned in?'

'I am sure he isn't,' I said.

He seemed to struggle with himself, for I heard something like the low, bitter murmur of doubt.

'What's the good?' His next words came out with a hesitating effort.

'Look here, my man. Could you call him out quietly?'

I thought the time had come to declare myself.

'*I* am the captain.'

I heard a 'By Jove!' whispered at the level of the water. The phosphorescence flashed in the swirl of the water all about his limbs, his other hand seized the ladder.

'My name's Leggatt.'

The voice was calm and resolute. A good voice. The self-possession of that man had somehow induced a corresponding state in myself. It was very quietly that I remarked:

'You must be a good swimmer.'

'Yes. I've been in the water practically since nine o'clock. The question for me now is whether I am to let go this ladder and go on swimming till I sink from exhaustion, or—to come on board here.'

I felt this was no mere formula of desperate speech, but a real alternative in the view of a strong soul. I should have gathered from this that he was young; indeed, it is only the young who are ever confronted by such clear issues. But at the time it was pure intuition on my part. A mysterious communication was established already between us two—in the face of that silent, darkened tropical sea. I was young, too; young enough to make no comment. The man in the water began suddenly to climb up the ladder, and I hastened away from the rail to fetch some clothes.

Before entering the cabin I stood still, listening in the lobby at the foot of the stairs. A faint snore came through the closed door of the chief mate's room. The second mate's door was on the hook, but the darkness in there was absolutely soundless. He, too, was young and could sleep like a stone. Remained the steward, but he was not likely to wake up before he was called. I got a sleeping-suit out of my room and, coming back on deck, saw the naked man from the sea sitting on the main-hatch, glimmering white in the darkness, his elbows on his knees and his head in his hands. In a moment he had concealed his damp body in a sleeping-suit of the same grey-stripe pattern as the one I was wearing and followed me like my double on the poop. Together we moved right aft, barefooted, silent.

'What is it?' I asked in a deadened voice, taking the lighted lamp out of the binnacle, and raising it to his face.

'An ugly business.'

He had rather regular features; a good mouth; light eyes under somewhat heavy, dark eyebrows; a smooth, square forehead; no growth on his cheeks; a small, brown moustache, and a well-shaped, round chin. His expression was concentrated, meditative, under the inspecting light of the lamp I held up to his face; such as a man thinking hard in solitude might wear. My sleeping-suit was just right for his size. A well-knit young fellow of twenty-five at most. He caught his lower lip with the edge of white, even teeth.

'Yes,' I said, replacing the lamp in the binnacle. The warm, heavy tropical night closed upon his head again.

'There's a ship over there,' he murmured.

'Yes, I know. The *Sephora*. Did you know of us?'

'Hadn't the slightest idea. I am the mate of her——' He paused and corrected himself. 'I should say I *was*.'

'Aha! Something wrong?'

'Yes. Very wrong indeed. I've killed a man.'

'What do you mean? Just now?'

'No, on the passage. Weeks ago. Thirty-nine south. When I say a man——'

'Fit of temper,' I suggested, confidently.

The shadowy, dark head, like mine, seemed to nod imperceptibly above the ghostly grey of my sleeping-suit. It was, in the night, as though I had been faced by my own reflection in the depths of a sombre and immense mirror.

'A pretty thing to have to own up to for a Conway boy', murmured my double, distinctly.

'You're a Conway boy?'

'I am,' he said, as if startled. Then, slowly . . . 'Perhaps you too——'

It was so; but being a couple of years older I had left before he joined. After a quick interchange of dates a silence fell; and I thought suddenly of my absurd mate with his terrific whiskers and the 'Bless my soul—you don't say so' type of intellect. My double gave me an inkling of his thoughts by saying: 'My father's a parson in Norfolk. Do you see me before a judge and jury on that charge? For myself I can't see the necessity. There are fellows that an angel from heaven——And I am not that. He was one of those creatures that are just simmering all the time with a silly sort of wickedness. Miserable devils that have no business to live at all. He wouldn't do his duty and wouldn't let anybody else do theirs. But what's the good of talking! You know well enough the sort of ill-conditioned snarling cur——'

He appealed to me as if our experiences had been as identical as our clothes. And I knew well enough the pestiferous danger of such a character where there are no means of legal repression. And I knew

well enough also that my double there was no homi-
cidal ruffian. I did not think of asking him for
details, and he told me the story roughly in brusque,
disconnected sentences. I needed no more. I saw it
all going on as though I were myself inside that other
sleeping-suit.

'It happened while we were setting a reefed foresail, at dusk. Reefed foresail! You understand the
sort of weather. The only sail we had left to keep
the ship running; so you may guess what it had been
like for days. Anxious sort of job, that. He gave me
some of his cursed insolence at the sheet. I tell you
I was overdone with this terrific weather that seemed
to have no end to it. Terrific, I tell you—and a deep
ship. I believe the fellow himself was half crazed with
funk. It was no time for gentlemanly reproof, so I
turned round and felled him like an ox. He up and
at me. We closed just as an awful sea made for the
ship. All hands saw it coming and took to the rigging, but I had him by the throat, and went on
shaking him like a rat, the men above us yelling,
"Look out! look out!" Then a crash as if the sky had
fallen on my head. They say that for over ten minutes hardly anything was to be seen of the ship—just
the three masts and a bit of the forecastle head and
of the poop all awash driving along in a smother of
foam. It was a miracle that they found us, jammed

together behind the forebits. It's clear that I meant business, because I was holding him by the throat still when they picked us up. He was black in the face. It was too much for them. It seems they rushed us aft together, gripped as we were, screaming "Murder!" like a lot of lunatics, and broke into the cuddy. And the ship running for her life, touch and go all the time, any minute her last in a sea fit to turn your hair grey only a-looking at it. I understand that the skipper, too, started raving like the rest of them. The man had been deprived of sleep for more than a week, and to have this sprung on him at the height of a furious gale nearly drove him out of his mind. I wonder they didn't fling me overboard after getting the carcass of their precious ship-mate out of my fingers. They had rather a job to separate us, I've been told. A sufficiently fierce story to make an old judge and a respectable jury sit up a bit. The first thing I heard when I came to myself was the maddening howling of that endless gale, and on that the voice of the old man. He was hanging on to my bunk, staring into my face out of his sou'wester.

'"Mr Leggatt, you have killed a man. You can act no longer as chief mate of this ship."'

His care to subdue his voice made it sound monotonous. He rested a hand on the end of the skylight to steady himself with, and all that time did not stir a limb, so far as I could see. 'Nice little tale for a quiet tea-party,' he concluded in the same tone.

One of my hands, too, rested on the end of the skylight; neither did I stir a limb, so far as I knew. We stood less than a foot from each other. It occurred to me that if old 'Bless my soul—you don't say so' were to put his head up the companion and catch sight of us, he would think he was seeing double, or imagine himself come upon a scene of weird witchcraft; the strange captain having a quiet confabulation by the wheel with his own grey ghost. I became very much concerned to prevent anything of the sort. I heard the other's soothing undertone.

'My father's a parson in Norfolk,' it said. Evidently he had forgotten he had told me this important fact before. Truly a nice little tale.

'You had better slip down into my stateroom now,' I said, moving off stealthily. My double followed my movements; our bare feet made no sound; I let him in, closed the door with care, and, after giving a call to the second mate, returned on deck for my relief.

'Not much sign of any wind yet,' I remarked when he approached.

'No, sir. Not much,' he assented, sleepily, in his hoarse voice, with just enough deference, no more, and barely suppressing a yawn.

'Well, that's all you have to look out for. You have got your orders.'

'Yes, sir.'

I paced a turn or two on the poop and saw him take up his position face forward with his elbow in the ratlines of the mizzen-rigging before I went below. The mate's faint snoring was still going on peacefully. The cuddy lamp was burning over the table on which stood a vase with flowers, a polite attention from the ship's provision merchant—the last flowers we should see for the next three months at the very least. Two bunches of bananas hung from the beam symmetrically, one on each side of the rudder-casing. Everything was as before in the ship—except that two of her captain's sleeping-suits were simultaneously in use, one motionless in the cuddy, the other keeping very still in the captain's stateroom.

It must be explained here that my cabin had the form of the capital letter L, the door being within the angle and opening into the short part of the letter. A couch was to the left, the bed-place to the right; my writing-desk and the chronometers' table faced the door. But anyone opening it, unless he stepped right inside, had no view of what I call the long (or vertical) part of the letter. It contained some lockers surmounted by a bookcase; and a few clothes, a thick jacket or two, caps, oilskin coat, and such like, hung on hooks. There was at the bottom of that part a door opening into my bathroom, which could be entered also directly from the saloon. But that way was never used.

The mysterious arrival had discovered the advantage of this particular shape. Entering my room, lighted strongly by a big bulkhead lamp swung on gimbals above my writing-desk, I did not see him anywhere till he stepped out quietly from behind the coats hung in the recessed part.

'I heard somebody moving about, and went in there at once,' he whispered.

I, too, spoke under my breath.

'Nobody is likely to come in here without knocking and getting permission.'

He nodded. His face was thin and the sunburn faded, as though he had been ill. And no wonder. He had been, I heard presently, kept under arrest in his cabin for nearly seven weeks. But there was nothing sickly in his eyes or in his expression. He was not a bit like me, really; yet, as we stood leaning over my bed-place, whispering side by side, with our dark heads together and our backs to the door, anybody bold enough to open it stealthily would have been treated to the uncanny sight of a double captain busy talking in whispers with his other self.

'But all this doesn't tell me how you came to hang on to our side-ladder,' I enquired, in the hardly audible murmurs we used, after he had told me something more of the proceedings on board the *Sephora* once the bad weather was over.

'When we sighted Java Head I had had time to think all those matters out several times over. I had six weeks of doing nothing else, and with only an hour or so every evening for a tramp on the quarterdeck.'

He whispered, his arms folded on the side of my bed-place, staring through the open port. And I could imagine perfectly the manner of this thinking out—a stubborn if not a steadfast operation; something of which I should have been perfectly incapable.

'I reckoned it would be dark, before we closed with the land,' he continued, so low that I had to strain my hearing, near as we were to each other, shoulder touching shoulder almost. 'So I asked to speak to the old man. He always seemed very sick when he came to see me—as if he could not look me in the face. You know, that foresail saved the ship. She was too deep to have run long under bare poles. And it was I that managed to set it for him. Anyway, he came. When I had him in my cabin—he stood by the door looking at me as if I had the halter round my neck already—I asked him right away to leave my cabin door unlocked at night while the ship was going through Sunda Straits. There would be the Java coast within two or three miles, off Angier Point. I wanted nothing more. I've had a prize for swimming my second year in the Conway.'

'I can believe it,' I breathed out.

'God only knows why they locked me in every night. To see some of their faces you'd have thought they were afraid I'd go about at night strangling people. Am I a murdering brute? Do I look it? By Jove! if I had been he wouldn't have trusted himself like that into my room. You'll say I might have chucked him aside and bolted out, there and then— it was dark already. Well, no. And for the same reason I wouldn't think of trying to smash the door. There would have been a rush to stop me at the noise, and I did not mean to get into a confounded scrimmage. Somebody else might have got killed— for I would not have broken out only to get chucked back, and I did not want any more of that work. He refused, looking more sick than ever. He was afraid of the men, and also of that old second mate of his who had been sailing with him for years—a grey-headed old humbug; and his steward, too, had been with him devil knows how long—seventeen years or more—a dogmatic sort of loafer who hated me like poison, just because I was the chief mate. No chief mate ever made more than one voyage in the *Sephora*, you know. Those two old chaps ran the ship. Devil only knows what the skipper wasn't afraid of (all his nerve went to pieces altogether in that hellish spell of bad weather we had)—of what the law would do to him—of his wife, perhaps. Oh, yes! she's on board. Though I don't think she would have meddled. She would have been only too glad to have me out of the ship in any way. The "brand of Cain" business, don't you see. That's all right. I was ready enough to go off wandering on the face of the earth—and that was price enough to pay for an Abel of that sort. Anyhow, he wouldn't listen to me. "This thing must take its course. I represent the law here." He was shaking like a leaf. "So you won't?" "No!" "Then I hope you will be able to sleep on that," I said, and turned my back on him. "I wonder that *you* can," cries he, and locks the door.

'Well, after that, I couldn't. Not very well. That was three weeks ago. We have had a slow passage through the Java Sea; drifted about Carimata for ten days. When we anchored here they thought, I suppose, it was all right. The nearest land (and that's five miles) is the ship's destination; the consul would soon set about catching me; and there would have been no object in bolting to these islets there. I don't suppose there's a drop of water on them. I don't know how it was, but tonight that steward, after bringing me my supper, went out to let me eat it, and left the door unlocked. And I ate it—all there was, too. After I had finished I strolled out on the quarter-deck. I don't know that I meant to do anything. A breath of fresh air was all I wanted, I believe. Then a sudden temptation came over me. I kicked off my slippers and was in the water before I had made up my mind fairly. Somebody heard the splash and they raised an awful hullabaloo. "He's gone! Lower the boats! He's committed suicide! No, he's swimming." Certainly I was swimming. It's not so easy for a swimmer like me to commit suicide by drowning. I landed on the nearest islet before the boat left the ship's side. I heard them pulling about in the dark, hailing, and so on, but after a bit they gave up. Everything quieted down and the anchorage became as still as death. I sat down on a stone and began to think. I felt certain they would start searching for me at daylight. There was no place to hide on those stony things—and if there had been, what would have been the good? But now I was clear of that ship, I was not going back. So after a while I took off all my clothes, tied them up in a bundle with a stone inside, and dropped them in the deep water on the outer side of that islet. That was suicide enough for me. Let them think what they liked, but I didn't mean to drown myself. I meant to swim till I sank—but that's not the same thing. I struck out for another of these little islands, and it was from that one that I first saw your riding-light. Something to swim for. I went on easily, and on the way I came upon a flat rock a foot or two above water. In the daytime, I dare say, you might make it out with a glass from your poop. I scrambled up on it and rested myself for a bit. Then I made another start. That last spell must have been over a mile.'

His whisper was getting fainter and fainter, and all the time he stared straight out through the port-hole, in which there was not even a star to be seen. I had not interrupted him. There was some-thing that made comment impossible in his narrative, or perhaps in himself; a sort of feeling, a quality, which I can't find a name for. And when he ceased, all I found was a futile whisper: 'So you swam for our light?'

'Yes—straight for it. It was something to swim for. I couldn't see any stars low down because the coast was in the way, and I couldn't see the land, either. The water was like glass. One might have been swimming in a confounded thousand-feet deep cistern with no place for scrambling out anywhere; but what I didn't like was the notion of swimming round and round like a crazed bullock before I gave out; and as I didn't mean to go back . . . No. Do you see me being hauled back, stark naked, off one of these little islands by the scruff of the neck and fighting like a wild beast? Somebody would have got killed for certain, and I did not want any of that. So I went on. Then your ladder——'

'Why didn't you hail the ship?' I asked, a link louder.

He touched my shoulder lightly. Lazy footsteps came right over our heads and stopped. The second mate had crossed from the other side of the poop and might have been hanging over the rail, for all we knew.

'He couldn't hear us talking—could he?' My double breathed into my very ear, anxiously.

His anxiety was an answer, a sufficient answer, to the question I had put to him. An answer containing all the difficulty of that situation. I closed the port-hole quietly, to make sure. A louder word might have been overheard.

'Who's that?' he whispered then.

'My second mate. But I don't know much more of the fellow than you do.'

And I told him a little about myself. I had been appointed to take charge while I least expected anything of the sort, not quite a fortnight ago. I didn't know either the ship or the people. Hadn't had the time in port to look about me or size anybody up. And as to the crew, all they knew was that I was appointed to take the ship home. For the rest, I was almost as much of a stranger on board as himself, I said. And at the moment I felt it most acutely. I felt that it would take very little to make me a suspect person in the eyes of the ship's company.

He had turned about meantime; and we, the two strangers in the ship, faced each other in identical attitudes.

'Your ladder——' he murmured, after a silence. 'Who'd have thought of finding a ladder hanging over at night in a ship anchored out here! I felt just then a very unpleasant faintness. After the life I've been leading for nine weeks, anybody would have got out of condition. I wasn't capable of swimming round as far as your rudder-chains. And, lo and behold! there was a ladder to get hold of. After I gripped it I said to myself, "What's the good?" When I saw a man's head looking over I thought I would swim away presently and leave him shouting—in whatever language it was. I didn't mind being looked at. I—I liked it. And then you speaking to me so quietly—as if you had expected me—made me hold on a little longer. It had been a confounded lonely time—I don't mean while swimming. I was glad to talk a little to somebody that didn't belong to the *Sephora*. As to asking for the captain, that was a mere impulse. It could have been no use, with all the ship knowing about me and the other people pretty certain to be round here in the morning. I don't know—I wanted to be seen, to talk with somebody, before I went on. I don't know what I would have said . . . "Fine night, isn't it?" or something of the sort.'

'Do you think they will be round here presently?' I asked with some incredulity.

'Quite likely', he said, faintly.

He looked extremely haggard all of a sudden. His head rolled on his shoulders.

'H'm. We shall see then. Meantime get into that bed', I whispered. 'Want help? There.'

It was a rather high bed-place with a set of drawers underneath. This amazing swimmer really needed the lift I gave him by seizing his leg. He tumbled in, rolled over on his back, and flung one arm across his eyes. And then, with his face nearly hidden, he must have looked exactly as I used to look in that bed. I gazed upon my other self for a while before drawing across carefully the two green serge curtains which ran on a brass rod. I thought for a moment of pinning them together for greater safety, but I sat down on the couch, and once there

I felt unwilling to rise and hunt for a pin. I would do it in a moment. I was extremely tired, in a peculiarly intimate way, by the strain of stealthiness, by the effort of whispering and the general secrecy of this excitement. It was three o'clock by now and I had been on my feet since nine, but I was not sleepy; I could not have gone to sleep. I sat there, fagged out, looking at the curtains, trying to clear my mind of the confused sensation of being in two places at once, and greatly bothered by an exasperating knocking in my head. It was a relief to discover suddenly that it was not in my head at all, but on the outside of the door. Before I could collect myself the words 'Come in' were out of my mouth, and the steward entered with a tray, bringing in my morning coffee. I had slept, after all, and I was so frightened that I shouted, 'This way! I am here, steward', as though he had been miles away. He put down the tray on the table next the couch and only then said, very quietly, 'I can see you are here, sir.' I felt him give me a keen look, but I dared not meet his eyes just then. He must have wondered why I had drawn the curtains of my bed before going to sleep on the couch. He went out, hooking the door open as usual.

I heard the crew washing decks above me. I knew I would have been told at once if there had been any wind. Calm, I thought, and I was doubly vexed.

Indeed, I felt dual more than ever. The steward reappeared suddenly in the doorway. I jumped up from the couch so quickly that he gave a start.

'What do you want here?'

'Close your port, sir—they are washing decks.'

'It is closed', I said, reddening.

'Very well, sir.' But he did not move from the doorway and returned my stare in an extraordinary, equivocal manner for a time. Then his eyes wavered, all his expression changed, and in a voice unusually gentle, almost coaxingly.

'May I come in to take the empty cup away, sir?'

'Of course!' I turned my back on him while he popped in and out. Then I unhooked and closed the door and even pushed the bolt. This sort of thing could not go on very long. The cabin was as hot as an oven, too. I took a peep at my double, and discovered that he had not moved, his arm was still over his eyes; but his chest heaved; his hair was wet; his chin glistened with perspiration. I reached over him and opened the port.

'I must show myself on deck,' I reflected.

Of course, theoretically, I could do what I liked, with no one to say nay to me within the whole circle of the horizon; but to lock my cabin door and take the key away I did not dare. Directly I put my head out of the companion I saw the group of my two officers, the second mate barefooted, the chief mate in long india-rubber boots, near the break of the poop, and the steward half-way down the poop-ladder talking to them eagerly. He happened to catch sight of me and dived, the second ran down on the main-deck shouting some order or other, and the chief mate came to meet me, touching his cap.

There was a sort of curiosity in his eye that I did not like. I don't know whether the steward had told them that I was 'queer' only, or downright drunk, but I know the man meant to have a good look at me. I watched him coming with a smile which, as he got into point-blank range, took effect and froze his very whiskers. I did not give him time to open his lips.

'Square the yards by lifts and braces before the hands go to breakfast.'

It was the first particular order I had given on board that ship; and I stayed on deck to see it executed, too. I had felt the need of asserting myself without loss of time. That sneering young cub got taken down a peg or two on that occasion, and I also seized the opportunity of having a good look at the face of every foremast man as they filed past me to go to the after braces. At breakfast time, eating nothing myself, I presided with such frigid dignity that the two mates were only too glad to escape from the cabin as soon as decency permitted; and all the time the dual working of my mind distracted me almost to the point of insanity. I was constantly watching myself, my secret self, as dependent on my actions as my own personality, sleeping in that bed, behind that door which faced me as I sat at the head of the table. It was very much like being mad, only it was worse because one was aware of it.

I had to shake him for a solid minute, but when at last he opened, his eyes it was in the full possession of his senses, with an enquiring look.

'All's well so far,' I whispered. 'Now you must vanish into the bathroom.'

He did so, as noiseless as a ghost, and then I rang for the steward, and facing him boldly, directed him to tidy up my stateroom while I was having my bath—'and be quick about it'. As my tone admitted of no excuses, he said, 'Yes, sir,' and ran off to fetch his dustpan and brushes. I took a bath and did most of my dressing, splashing, and whistling softly for the steward's edification, while the secret sharer of my life stood drawn up bolt upright in that little space, his face looking very sunken in daylight, his eyelids lowered under the stern, dark line of his eyebrows drawn together by a slight frown.

When I left him there to go back to my room the steward was finishing dusting. I sent for the mate and engaged him in some insignificant conversation. It was, as it were, trifling with the terrific character of his whiskers; but my object was to give him an opportunity for a good look at my cabin. And then I could at last shut, with a clear conscience, the door of my stateroom and get my double back into the recessed part. There was nothing else for it. He had to sit still on a small folding stool, half smothered by the heavy coats hanging there. We listened to the steward going into the bathroom out of the saloon, filling the water-bottles there, scrubbing the bath, setting things to rights, whisk, bang, clatter—out again into the saloon—turn the key—click. Such was my scheme for keeping my second self invisible. Nothing better could be contrived under the circumstances. And there we sat; I at my writing-desk ready to appear busy with some papers, he behind me out of sight of the door. It would not have been prudent to talk in daytime; and I could not have stood the excitement of that queer sense of whispering to myself. Now and then, glancing over my shoulder, I saw him far back there, sitting rigidly on the low stool, his bare feet close together, his arms folded, his head hanging on his breast—and perfectly still. Anybody would have taken him for me.

I was fascinated by it myself. Every moment I

had to glance over my shoulder. I was looking at him when a voice outside the door said:

'Beg pardon, sir.'

'Well!' . . . I kept my eyes on him, and so when the voice outside the door announced, 'There's a ship's boat coming our way, sir,' I saw him give a start—the first movement he had made for hours. But he did not raise his bowed head.

'All right. Get the ladder over.'

I hesitated. Should I whisper something to him? But what? His immobility seemed to have been never disturbed. What could I tell him he did not know already? . . . Finally I went on deck.

II

The skipper of the *Sephora* had a thin red whisker all round his face, and the sort of complexion that goes with hair of that colour, also the particular, rather smeary shade of blue in the eyes. He was not exactly a showy figure; his shoulders were high, his stature but middling—one leg slightly more bandy than the other. He shook hands, looking vaguely around. A spiritless tenacity was his main characteristic, I judged. I behaved with a politeness which seemed to disconcert him. Perhaps he was shy. He mumbled to me as if he were ashamed of what he was saying; gave his name (it was something like Archbold—but at this distance of years I hardly am sure), his ship's name, and a few other particulars of that sort, in the manner of a criminal making a reluctant and doleful confession. He had had terrible weather on the passage out—terrible—terrible—wife aboard, too.

By this time we were seated in the cabin and the steward brought in a tray with a bottle and glasses. 'Thanks! No.' Never took liquor. Would have some water, though. He drank two tumblerfuls. Terrible thirsty work. Ever since daylight had been exploring the islands round his ship.

'What was that for—fun?' I asked, with an appearance of polite interest.

'No!' He sighed. 'Painful duty.'

As he persisted in his mumbling and I wanted my double to hear every word, I hit upon the notion of informing him that I regretted to say I was hard of hearing.

'Such a young man, too!' he nodded, keeping his smeary blue, unintelligent eyes fastened upon me. What was the cause of it—some disease? he enquired, without the least sympathy and as if he thought that, if so, I'd got no more than I deserved.

'Yes; disease,' I admitted in a cheerful tone which seemed to shock him. But my point was gained, because he had to raise his voice to give me his tale. It is not worthwhile to record that version. It was just over two months since all this had happened, and he had thought so much about it that he seemed completely muddled as to its bearings, but still immensely impressed.

'What would you think of such a thing happening on board your own ship? I've had the *Sephora* for these fifteen years. I am a well-known shipmaster.'

He was densely distressed—and perhaps I should have sympathized with him if I had been able to detach my mental vision from the unsuspected sharer of my cabin as though he were my second self. There he was on the other side of the bulkhead, four or five feet from us, no more, as we sat in the saloon. I looked politely at Captain Archbold (if that was his name), but it was the other I saw, in a grey sleeping-suit, seated on a low stool, his bare feet close together, his arms folded, and every word said between us falling into the ears of his dark head bowed on his chest.

'I have been at sea now, man and boy, for seven-and-thirty years, and I've never heard of such a thing happening in an English ship. And that it should be my ship. Wife on board, too.'

I was hardly listening to him.

'Don't you think', I said, 'that the heavy sea which, you told me, came aboard just then might have killed the man? I have seen the sheer weight of a sea kill a man very neatly, by simply breaking his neck.'

'Good God!' he uttered, impressively, fixing his smeary blue eyes on me. 'The sea! No man killed by the sea ever looked like that.' He seemed positively scandalized at my suggestion. And as I gazed at him, certainly not prepared for anything original on his part, he advanced his head close to mine and thrust his tongue out at me so suddenly that I couldn't help starting back.

After scoring over my calmness in this graphic way he nodded wisely. If I had seen the sight, he assured me, I would never forget it as long as I lived. The weather was too bad to give the corpse a proper sea burial. So next day at dawn they took it up on the poop, covering its face with a bit of bunting; he read a short prayer, and then, just as it was, in its oilskins and long boots, they launched it amongst those mountainous seas that seemed ready every moment to swallow up the ship herself and the terrified lives on board of her.

'That reefed foresail saved you', I threw in.

'Under God—it did,' he exclaimed fervently. 'It was by a special mercy, I firmly believe, that it stood some of those hurricane squalls.'

'It was the setting of that sail which——' I began.

'God's own hand in it,' he interrupted me.

'Nothing less could have done it. I don't mind telling you that I hardly dared give the order. It seemed impossible that we could touch anything without losing it, and then our last hope would have been gone.'

The terror of that gale was on him yet. I let him go on for a bit, then said, casually—as if returning to a minor subject:

'You were very anxious to give up your mate to the shore people, I believe?'

He was. To the law. His obscure tenacity on that point had in it something incomprehensible and a little awful; something, as it were, mystical, quite apart from his anxiety that he should not be suspected of 'countenancing any doings of that sort'. Seven-and-thirty virtuous years at sea, of which over twenty of immaculate command, and the last fifteen in the *Sephora*, seemed to have laid him under some pitiless obligation.

'And you know', he went on, groping shamefacedly amongst his feelings, 'I did not engage that young fellow. His people had some interest with my owners. I was in a way forced to take him on. He looked very smart, very gentlemanly, and all that. But do you know—I never liked him, somehow. I am a plain man. You see, he wasn't exactly the sort for the chief mate of a ship like the *Sephora*.'

I had become so connected in thoughts and impressions with the secret sharer of my cabin that I felt as if I, personally, were being given to understand that I, too, was not the sort that would have done for the chief mate of a ship like the *Sephora*. I had no doubt of it in my mind.

'Not at all the style of man. You understand,' he insisted, superfluously, looking hard at me.

I smiled urbanely. He seemed at a loss for a while.

'I suppose I must report a suicide.'

'Beg pardon?'

'Sui-cide! That's what I'll have to write to my owners directly I get in.'

'Unless you manage to recover him before tomorrow', I assented, dispassionately. . . . 'I mean, alive.'

He mumbled something which I really did not catch, and I turned my ear to him in a puzzled manner. He fairly bawled:

'The land—I say, the mainland is at least seven miles off my anchorage.'

'About that.'

My lack of excitement, of curiosity, of surprise, of any sort of pronounced interest, began to arouse his distrust. But except for the felicitous pretence of deafness I had not tried to pretend anything. I had felt utterly incapable of playing the part of ignorance properly, and therefore was afraid to try. It is also certain that he had brought some ready-made suspicions with him, and that he viewed my politeness as a strange and unnatural phenomenon. And yet how else could I have received him? Not heartily! That was impossible for psychological reasons, which I need not state here. My only object was to keep off his enquiries. Surlily? Yes, but surliness might have provoked a point-blank question. From its novelty to him and from its nature, punctilious courtesy was the manner best calculated to restrain the man. But there was the danger of his breaking through my defence bluntly. I could not, I think, have met him by a direct lie, also for psychological (not moral) reasons. If he had only known how afraid I was of his putting my feeling of identity with the other to the test! But, strangely enough—(I thought of it only afterwards)—I believe that he was not a little disconcerted by the reverse side of that weird situation, by something in me that reminded him of the man he was seeking—suggested a mysterious similitude to the young fellow he had distrusted and disliked from the first.

However that might have been, the silence was not very prolonged. He took another oblique step.

'I reckon I had no more than a two-mile pull to your ship. Not a bit more.'

'And quite enough, too, in this awful heat,' I said.

Another pause full of mistrust followed. Necessity, they say, is mother of invention, but fear, too, is not barren of ingenious suggestions. And I was afraid he would ask me point-blank for news of my other self.

'Nice little saloon, isn't it?' I remarked, as if noticing for the first time the way his eyes roamed from one closed door to the other. 'And very well fitted out, too. Here, for instance', I continued, reaching over the back of my seat negligently and flinging the door open, 'is my bathroom.'

He made an eager movement, but hardly gave it a glance. I got up, shut the door of the bathroom, and invited him to have a look round, as if I were very proud of my accommodation. He had to rise and be shown round, but he went through the business without any raptures whatever.

'And now we'll have a look at my stateroom,' I declared, in a voice as loud as I dared to make it, crossing the cabin to the starboard side with purposely heavy steps.

He followed me in and gazed around. My intelligent double had vanished. I played my part.

'Very convenient—isn't it?'

'Very nice. Very comf . . .' He didn't finish and went out brusquely as if to escape from some

unrighteous wiles of mine. But it was not to be. I
had been too frightened not to feel vengeful; I felt I
had him on the run, and I meant to keep him on the
run. My polite insistence must have had something
menacing in it, because he gave in suddenly. And I
did not let him off a single item; mate's room,
pantry, storerooms, the very sail-locker which was
also under the poop—he had to look into them all.
When at last I showed him out on the quarterdeck
he drew a long, spiritless sigh, and mumbled dis-
mally that he must really be going back to his ship
now. I desired my mate, who had joined us, to see
to the captain's boat.

The man of whiskers gave a blast on the whistle
which he used to wear hanging round his neck, and
yelled, '*Sephora*'s away!' My double down there in
my cabin must have heard, and certainly could not
feel more relieved than I. Four fellows came running
out from somewhere forward and went over the side,
while my own men, appearing on deck too, lined the
rail. I escorted my visitor to the gangway ceremoni-
ously, and nearly overdid it. He was a tenacious
beast. On the very ladder he lingered, and in that
unique, guiltily conscientious manner of sticking to
the point:

'I say . . . you . . . you don't think that——'

I covered his voice loudly:

'Certainly not . . . I am delighted. Goodbye.'

I had an idea of what he meant to say, and just saved myself by the privilege of defective hearing. He was too shaken generally to insist, but my mate, close witness of that parting, looked mystified and his face took on a thoughtful cast. As I did not want to appear as if I wished to avoid all communication with my officers, he had the opportunity to address me.

'Seems a very nice man. His boat's crew told our chaps a very extraordinary story, if what I am told by the steward is true. I suppose you had it from the captain, sir?'

'Yes. I had a story from the captain.'

'A very horrible affair—isn't it, sir?'

'It is.'

'Beats all these tales we hear about murders in Yankee ships.'

'I don't think it beats them. I don't think it resembles them in the least.'

'Bless my soul—you don't say so! But of course I've no acquaintance whatever with American ships, not I, so I couldn't go against your knowledge. It's horrible enough for me . . . But the queerest part is that those fellows seemed to have some idea the man was hidden aboard here. They had really. Did you ever hear of such a thing?'

'Preposterous—isn't it?'

We were walking to and fro athwart the quarter-deck. No one of the crew forward could be seen (the day was Sunday), and the mate pursued:

'There was some little dispute about it. Our chaps took offence. "As if we would harbour a thing like that", they said. "Wouldn't you like to look for him in our coal-hole?" Quite a tiff. But they made it up in the end. I suppose he did drown himself. Don't you, sir?'

'I don't suppose anything.'

'You have no doubt in the matter, sir?'

'None whatever.'

I left him suddenly. I felt I was producing a bad impression, but with my double down there it was most trying to be on deck. And it was almost as trying to be below. Altogether a nerve-trying situation. But on the whole I felt less torn in two when I was with him. There was no one in the whole ship whom I dared take into my confidence. Since the hands had got to know his story, it would have been impossible to pass him off for anyone else, and an accidental discovery was to be dreaded now more than ever . . .

The steward being engaged in laying the table for dinner, we could talk only with our eyes when I first went down. Later in the afternoon we had a cautious try at whispering. The Sunday quietness of the ship was against us; the stillness of air and water around her was against us; the elements, the men were against us—everything was against us in our secret partnership; time itself—for this could not go on forever. The very trust in Providence was, I suppose, denied to his guilt. Shall I confess that this thought cast me down very much? And as to the chapter of accidents which counts for so much in the book of success, I could only hope that it was closed. For what favourable accident could be expected?

'Did you hear everything?' were my first words as soon as we took up our position side by side, leaning over my bed-place.

He had. And the proof of it was his earnest whisper, 'The man told you he hardly dared to give the order.'

I understood the reference to be to that saving foresail.

'Yes. He was afraid of it being lost in the setting.'

'I assure you he never gave the order. He may think he did, but he never gave it. He stood there with me on the break of the poop after the maintopsail blew away, and whimpered about our last hope—positively whimpered about it and nothing else—and the night coming on! To hear one's skipper go on like that in such weather was enough to drive any fellow out of his mind. It worked me up into a sort of desperation. I just took it into my own hands and went away from him, boiling, and—But what's the use telling you? *You* know! . . . Do you think that if I had not been pretty fierce with them I should have got the men to do anything? Not it! The bo's'n perhaps? Perhaps! It wasn't a heavy sea—it was a sea gone mad! I suppose the end of the world will be something like that; and a man may have the heart to see it coming once and be done with it—but to have to face it day after day—I don't blame anybody. I was precious little better than the rest. Only—I was an officer of that old coal-wagon, anyhow——'

'I quite understand,' I conveyed that sincere assurance into his ear. He was out of breath with whispering; I could hear him pant slightly. It was all very simple. The same strung-up force which had given twenty-four men a chance, at least, for their lives, had, in a sort of recoil, crushed an unworthy mutinous existence.

But I had no leisure to weigh the merits of the matter—footsteps in the saloon, a heavy knock 'There's enough wind to get under way with, sir.' Here was the call of a new claim upon my thoughts and even upon my feelings.

'Turn the hands up,' I cried through the door. 'I'll be on deck directly.'

I was going out to make the acquaintance of my ship. Before I left the cabin our eyes met—the eyes of the only two strangers on board. I pointed to the recessed part where the little camp-stool awaited him and hid my finger on my lips. He made a gesture—somewhat vague—a little mysterious, accompanied by a faint smile, as if of regret.

This is not the place to enlarge upon the sensations of a man who feels for the first time a ship move under his feet to his own independent word. In my case they were not unalloyed. I was not wholly alone with my command; for there was that stranger in my cabin. Or rather, I was not completely and wholly with her. Part of me was absent. That mental feeling of being in two places at once affected me physically as if the mood of secrecy had penetrated my very soul. Before an hour had elapsed since the ship had begun to move, having occasion to ask the mate (he stood by my side) to take a compass bearing of the Pagoda, I caught myself reaching up to his ear in whispers. I say I caught myself, but enough had escaped to startle the man. I can't describe it otherwise than by saying that he shied. A grave, pre-occupied manner, as though he were in possession of some perplexing intelligence, did not leave him henceforth. A little later I moved away from the rail to look at the compass with such a stealthy gait that the helmsman noticed it—and I could not help noticing the unusual roundness of his eyes. These are trifling instances, though it's to no commander's advantage to be suspected of ludicrous eccentricities. But I was also more seriously affected. There are to a seaman certain words, gestures, that should in given conditions come as naturally, as instinctively as the winking of a menaced eye. A certain order should spring on to his lips without thinking; a certain sign should get itself made, so to speak, without reflection. But all unconscious alertness had abandoned me. I had to make an effort of will to recall myself back (from the cabin) to the conditions of the moment. I felt that I was appearing an irresolute commander to those people who were watching me more or less critically.

And, besides, there were the scares. On the second day out, for instance, coming off the deck in the afternoon (I had straw slippers on my bare feet) I stopped at the open pantry door and spoke to the steward. He was doing something there with his back to me. At the sound of my voice he nearly jumped out of his skin, as the saying is, and incidentally broke a cup.

'What on earth's the matter with you?' I asked, astonished.

He was extremely confused. 'Beg your pardon, sir. I made sure you were in your cabin.'

'You see I wasn't.'

'No, sir. I could have sworn I had heard you moving in there not a moment ago. It's most extraordinary . . . very sorry, sir.'

I passed on with an inward shudder. I was so identified with my secret double that I did not even mention the fact in those scanty, fearful whispers we exchanged. I suppose he had made some slight noise of some kind or other. It would have been miraculous if he hadn't at one time or another. And yet, haggard as he appeared, he looked always perfectly self-controlled, more than calm—almost invulnerable. On my suggestion he remained almost entirely in the bathroom, which, upon the whole, was the safest place. There could be really no shadow of an excuse for anyone ever wanting to go in there, once the steward had done with it. It was a very tiny place. Sometimes he reclined on the floor, his legs bent, his head sustained on one elbow. At others I would find him on the camp-stool, sitting in his grey sleeping-suit and with his cropped dark hair like a patient, unmoved convict. At night I would smuggle him into my bed-place, and we would whisper together, with the regular footfalls of the officer of the watch passing and repassing over our heads. It was an infinitely miserable time. It was lucky that some tins of fine preserves were stowed in a locker in my stateroom; hard bread I could always get hold of; and so he lived on stewed chicken, paté de foie gras, asparagus, cooked oysters, sardines—on all sorts of abominable sham delicacies out of tins. My early morning coffee he always drank; and it was all I dared do for him in that respect.

Every day there was the horrible manœuvring to go through so that my room and then the bathroom should be done in the usual way. I came to hate the sight of the steward, to abhor the voice of that harmless man. I felt that it was he who would bring on the disaster of discovery. It hung like a sword over our heads.

The fourth day out, I think (we were then working down the east side of the Gulf of Siam, tack for tack, in light winds and smooth water)—the fourth day, I say, of this miserable juggling with the unavoidable, as we sat at our evening meal, that man, whose slightest movement I dreaded, after putting down the dishes ran up on deck busily. This could not be dangerous. Presently he came down again; and then it appeared that he had remembered a coat of mine which I had thrown over a rail to dry after having been wetted in a shower which had passed over the ship in the afternoon. Sitting stolidly at the head of the table I became terrified at the sight of the garment on his arm. Of course he made for my door. There was no time to lose.

'Steward,' I thundered. My nerves were so shaken that I could not govern my voice and conceal my agitation. This was the sort of thing that made my terrifically whiskered mate tap his forehead with his forefinger. I had detected him using that gesture while talking on deck with a confidential air to the carpenter. It was too far to hear a word, but I had no doubt that this pantomime could only refer to the strange new captain.

'Yes, sir,' the pale-faced steward turned resignedly to me. It was this maddening course of being shouted at, checked without rhyme or reason, arbitrarily chased out of my cabin, suddenly called into it, sent flying out of his pantry on incomprehensible errands, that accounted for the growing wretchedness of his expression.

'Where are you going with that coat?'

'To your room, sir.'

'Is there another shower coming?'

'I'm sure I don't know, sir. Shall I go up again and see, sir?'

'No! never mind.'

My object was attained, as of course my other self in there would have heard everything that passed. During this interlude my two officers never raised their eyes off their respective plates; but the lip of that confounded cub, the second mate, quivered visibly.

I expected the steward to hook my coat on and come out at once. He was very slow about it; but I dominated my nervousness sufficiently not to shout after him. Suddenly I became aware (it could be heard plainly enough) that the fellow for some reason or other was opening the door of the bathroom. It was the end. The place was literally not big enough to swing a cat in. My voice died in my throat and I went stony all over. I expected to hear a yell of surprise and terror, and made a movement, but had not the strength to get on my legs. Everything remained still. Had my second self taken the poor wretch by the throat? I don't know what I could have done next moment if I had not seen the steward come out of my room, close the door, and then stand quietly by the sideboard.

'Saved,' I thought. 'But, no! Lost! Gone! He was gone!'

I laid my knife and fork down and leaned back in my chair. My head swam. After a while, when sufficiently recovered to speak in a steady voice, I instructed my mate to put the ship round at eight o'clock himself.

'I won't come on deck,' I went on. 'I think I'll turn in, and unless the wind shifts I don't want to be disturbed before midnight. I feel a bit seedy.'

'You did look middling bad a little while ago,' the chief mate remarked without showing any great concern.

They both went out, and I stared at the steward clearing the table. There was nothing to be read on that wretched man's face. But why did he avoid my eyes I asked myself. Then I thought I should like to hear the sound of his voice.

'Steward!'

'Sir!' Startled as usual.

'Where did you hang up that coat?'

'In the bathroom, sir.' The usual anxious tone. 'It's not quite dry yet, sir.'

For some time longer I sat in the cuddy. Had my double vanished as he had come? But of his coming there was an explanation, whereas his disappearance would be inexplicable . . . I went slowly into my dark room, shut the door, lighted the lamp, and for a time dared not turn round. When at last I did I saw him standing bolt-upright in the narrow recessed part. It would not be true to say I had a shock, but an irresistible doubt of his bodily existence flitted through my mind. Can it be, I asked myself, that he is not visible to other eyes than mine? It was like being haunted. Motionless, with a grave face, he raised his hands slightly at me in a gesture which meant clearly, 'Heavens! what a narrow escape!' Narrow indeed. I think I had come creeping quietly as near insanity as any man who has not actually gone over the border. That gesture restrained me, so to speak.

The mate with the terrific whiskers was now putting the ship on the other tack. In the moment of profound silence which follows upon the hands going to their stations I heard on the poop his raised voice: 'Hard alee!' and the distant shout of the order repeated on the main deck. The sails, in that light breeze, made but a faint fluttering noise. It ceased. The ship was coming round slowly; I held my breath in the renewed stillness of expectation; one wouldn't have thought that there was a single living soul on her decks. A sudden brisk shout, 'Mainsail haul!' broke the spell, and in the noisy cries and rush overhead of the men running away with the main-brace we two, down in my cabin, came together in our usual position by the bed-place.

He did not wait for my question. 'I heard him fumbling here and just managed to squat myself down in the bath,' he whispered to me. 'The fellow only opened the door and put his arm in to hang the coat up. All the same——'

'I never thought of that,' I whispered back, even

more appalled than before at the closeness of the shave, and marvelling at that something unyielding in his character which was carrying him through so finely. There was no agitation in his whisper. Whoever was being driven distracted, it was not he. He was sane. And the proof of his sanity was continued when he took up the whispering again.

'It would never do for me to come to life again.'

It was something that a ghost might have said. But what he was alluding to was his old captain's reluctant admission of the theory of suicide. It would obviously serve his turn—if I had understood at all the view which seemed to govern the unalterable purpose of his action.

'You must maroon me as soon as ever you can get amongst these islands off the Cambodje shore,' he went on.

'Maroon you! We are not living in a boy's adventure tale,' I protested. His scornful whispering took me up.

'We aren't indeed! There's nothing of a boy's tale in this. But there's nothing else for it. I want no more. You don't suppose I am afraid of what can be done to me? Prison or gallows or whatever they may please. But you don't see me coming back to explain such things to an old fellow in a wig and twelve respectable tradesmen, do you? What can they know whether I am guilty or not—or of *what* I am guilty, either? That's my affair. What does the Bible say? "Driven off the face of the earth." Very well. I am off the face of the earth now. As I came at night so I shall go.'

'Impossible!' I murmured. 'You can't.'

'Can't? . . . Not naked like a soul on the Day of Judgement. I shall freeze on to this sleeping-suit. The Last Day is not yet—and . . . you have understood thoroughly. Didn't you?'

I felt suddenly ashamed of myself. I may say truly that I understood—and my hesitation in letting that man swim away from my ship's side had been a mere sham sentiment, a sort of cowardice.

'It can't be done now till next night,' I breathed out. 'The ship is on the off-shore tack and the wind may fail us.'

'As long as I know that you understand,' he whispered. 'But of course you do. It's a great satisfaction to have got somebody to understand. You seem to have been there on purpose.' And in the same whisper, as if we two whenever we talked had to say things to each other which were not fit for the world to hear, he added, 'It's very wonderful.'

We remained side by side talking in our secret way—but sometimes silent or just exchanging a whispered word or two at long intervals. And as usual he stared through the port. A breath of wind came now and again into our faces. The ship might have been moored in dock, so gently and on an even keel she slipped through the water, that did not murmur even at our passage, shadowy and silent like a phantom sea.

At midnight I went on deck, and to my mate's great surprise put the ship round on the other tack. His terrible whiskers flitted round me in silent criticism. I certainly should not have done it if it had been only a question of getting out of that sleepy gulf as quickly as possible. I believe he told the second mate, who relieved him, that it was a great want of judgement. The other only yawned. That intolerable cub shuffled about so sleepily and lolled against the rails in such a slack, improper fashion that I came down on him sharply.

'Aren't you properly awake yet?'

'Yes, sir! I am awake.'

'Well, then, be good enough to hold yourself as if you were. And keep a look-out. If there's any current we'll be closing with some islands before daylight.'

The east side of the gulf is fringed with islands, some solitary, others in groups. On the blue background of the high coast they seem to float on silvery patches of calm water, arid and grey, or dark green and rounded like clumps of evergreen bushes, with the larger ones, a mile or two long, showing the outlines of ridges, ribs of grey rock under the dank mantle of matted leafage. Unknown to trade, to travel, almost to geography, the manner of life they harbour is an unsolved secret. There must be villages—settlements of fishermen at least—on the largest of them, and some communication with the world is probably kept up by native craft. But all that forenoon, as we headed for them, fanned along by the faintest of breezes, I saw no sign of man or canoe in the field of the telescope I kept on pointing at the scattered group.

At noon I gave no orders for a change of course, and the mate's whiskers became much concerned and seemed to be offering themselves unduly to my notice. At last I said:

'I am going to stand right in. Quite in—as far as I can take her.'

The stare of extreme surprise imparted an air of ferocity also to his eyes, and he looked truly terrific for a moment.

'We're not doing well in the middle of the gulf,' I continued, casually. 'I am going to look for the land breezes tonight.'

'Bless my soul! Do you mean, sir, in the dark amongst the lot of all them islands and reefs and shoals?'

'Well—if there are any regular land breezes at all on this coast one must get close inshore to find them, mustn't one?'

'Bless my soul!' he exclaimed again under his breath. All that afternoon he wore a dreamy, contemplative appearance which in him was a mark of perplexity. After dinner I went into my stateroom as if I meant to take some rest. There we two bent our dark heads over a half-unrolled chart lying on my bed.

'There,' I said. 'It's got to be Koh-ring. I've been looking at it ever since sunrise. It has got two hills and a low point. It must be inhabited. And on the coast opposite there is what looks like the mouth of a biggish river—with some town, no doubt, not far up. It's the best chance for you that I can see.'

'Anything. Koh-ring let it be.'

He looked thoughtfully at the chart as if surveying chances and distances from a lofty height—and following with his eyes his own figure wandering on the blank land of Cochin-China, and then passing off that piece of paper clean out of sight into uncharted regions. And it was as if the ship had two captains to plan her course for her. I had been so worried and restless running up and down that I had not had the patience to dress that day. I had remained in my sleeping-suit, with straw slippers and a soft floppy hat. The closeness of the heat in the gulf had been most oppressive, and the crew were used to seeing me wandering in that airy attire.

'She will clear the south point as she heads now,' I whispered into his ear. 'Goodness only knows when, though, but certainly after dark. I'll edge her in to half a mile, as far as I may be able to judge in the dark——'

'Be careful,' he murmured, warningly—and I realized suddenly that all my future, the only future for which I was fit, would perhaps go irretrievably to pieces in any mishap to my first command.

I could not stop a moment longer in the room. I motioned him to get out of sight and made my way on the poop. That unplayful cub had the watch. I walked up and down for a while thinking things out, then beckoned him over.

'Send a couple of hands to open the two quarter-deck ports,' I said, mildly.

He actually had the impudence, or else so forgot himself in his wonder at such an incomprehensible order, as to repeat:

'Open the quarterdeck ports! What for, sir?'

'The only reason you need concern yourself about is because I tell you to do so. Have them open wide and fastened properly.'

He reddened and went off, but I believe made

some jeering remark to the carpenter as to the sensible practice of ventilating a ship's quarterdeck. I know he popped into the mate's cabin to impart the fact to him because the whiskers came on deck, as it were by chance, and stole glances at me from below—for signs of lunacy or drunkenness, I suppose.

A little before supper, feeling more restless than ever, I rejoined, for a moment, my second self. And to find him sitting so quietly was surprising, like something against nature, inhuman.

I developed my plan in a hurried whisper.

'I shall stand in as close as I dare and then put her round. I will presently find means to smuggle you out of here into the sail-locker, which communicates with the lobby. But there is an opening, a sort of square for hauling the sails out, which gives straight on the quarterdeck and which is never closed in fine weather, so as to give air to the sails. When the ship's way is deadened in stays and all the hands are aft at the main-braces you will have a clear road to slip out and get overboard through the open quarterdeck port. I've had them both fastened up. Use a rope's end to lower yourself into the water so as to avoid a splash—you know. It could be heard and cause some beastly complication.'

He kept silent for a while, then whispered, 'I understand.'

'I won't be there to see you go,' I began with an effort. 'The rest . . . I only hope I have understood, too.'

'You have. From first to last'—and for the first time there seemed to be a faltering, something strained in his whisper. He caught hold of my arm, but the ringing of the supper bell made me start. He didn't, though; he only released his grip.

After supper I didn't come below again till well past eight o'clock. The faint, steady breeze was loaded with dew; and the wet, darkened sails held all there was of propelling power in it. The night, clear and starry, sparkled darkly, and the opaque, lightless patches shifting slowly against the low stars were the drifting islets. On the port bow there was a big one more distant and shadowily imposing by the great space of sky it eclipsed.

On opening the door I had a back view of my very own self looking at a chart. He had come out of the recess and was standing near the table.

'Quite dark enough,' I whispered.

He stepped back and leaned against my bed with a level, quiet glance. I sat on the couch. We had nothing to say to each other. Over our heads the officer of the watch moved here and there. Then I heard him move quickly. I knew what that meant. He was making for the companion; and presently his voice was outside my door.

'We are drawing in pretty fast, sir. Land looks rather close.'

'Very well,' I answered. 'I am coming on deck directly.'

I waited till he was gone out of the cuddy, then rose. My double moved too. The time had come to exchange our last whispers, for neither of us was ever to hear each other's natural voice.

'Look here!' I opened a drawer and took out three sovereigns. 'Take this anyhow. I've got six and I'd give you the lot, only I must keep a little money to buy some fruit and vegetables for the crew from native boats as we go through Sunda Straits.'

He shook his head.

'Take it,' I urged him, whispering desperately. 'No one can tell what——'

He smiled and slapped meaningly the only pocket of the sleeping-jacket. It was not safe, certainly. But I produced a large old silk handkerchief of mine, and tying the three pieces of gold in a comer, pressed it on him. He was touched, I suppose, because he took it at last and tied it quickly round his waist under the jacket, on his bare skin.

Our eyes met; several seconds elapsed, till, our

glances still mingled, I extended my hand and turned the lamp out. Then I passed through the cuddy, leaving the door of my room wide open. . . . 'Steward!'

He was still lingering in the pantry in the greatness of his zeal, giving a rub-up to a plated cruet stand the last thing before going to bed. Being careful not to wake up the mate, whose room was opposite, I spoke in an undertone.

He looked round anxiously. 'Sir!'

'Can you get me a little hot water from the galley?'

'I am afraid, sir, the galley fire's been out for some time now.'

'Go and see.'

He flew up the stairs.

'Now,' I whispered, loudly, into the saloon—too loudly, perhaps, but I was afraid I couldn't make a sound. He was by my side in an instant—the double captain slipped past the stairs—through a tiny dark passage . . . a sliding door. We were in the sail-locker, scrambling on our knees over the sails. A sudden thought struck me. I saw myself wandering barefooted, bareheaded, the sun beating on my dark poll. I snatched off my floppy hat and tried hurriedly in the dark to ram it on my other self. He dodged and fended off silently. I wonder what he thought had come to me before he understood and suddenly desisted. Our hands met gropingly, lingered united in a steady, motionless clasp for a second. . . . No word was breathed by either of us when they separated.

I was standing quietly by the pantry door when the steward returned.

'Sorry, sir. Kettle barely warm. Shall I light the spirit-lamp?'

'Never mind.'

I came out on deck slowly. It was now a matter of conscience to shave the land as close as possible—for now he must go overboard whenever the ship was put in stays. Must! There could be no going back for him. After a moment I walked over to leeward and my heart flew into my mouth at the nearness of the land on the bow. Under any other circumstances I would not have held on a minute longer. The second mate had followed me anxiously.

I looked on till I felt I could command my voice.

'She may weather,' I said then in a quiet tone.

'Are you going to try that, sir?' he stammered out incredulously.

I took no notice of him and raised my tone just enough to be heard by the helmsman.

'Keep her good full.'

'Good full, sir.'

The wind fanned my cheek, the sails slept, the world was silent. The strain of watching the dark loom of the land grow bigger and denser was too much for me. I had shut my eyes—because the ship must go closer. She must! The stillness was intolerable. Were we standing still?

When I opened my eyes the second view started my heart with a thump. The black southern hill of Koh-ring seemed to hang right over the ship like a towering fragment of the everlasting night. On that enormous mass of blackness there was not a gleam to be seen, not a sound to be heard. It was gliding irresistibly towards us and yet seemed already within reach of the hand. I saw the vague figures of the watch grouped in the waist, gazing in awed silence.

'Are you going on, sir?' enquired an unsteady voice at my elbow.

I ignored it. I had to go on.

'Keep her full. Don't check her way. That won't do now,' I said, warningly.

'I can't see the sails very well,' the helmsman answered me, in strange, quavering tones.

Was she close enough? Already she was, I won't say in the shadow of the land, but in the very blackness of it, already swallowed up as it were, gone too close to be recalled, gone from me altogether.

'Give the mate a call,' I said to the young man

who stood at my elbow as still as death. 'And turn all hands up.'

My tone had a borrowed loudness reverberated from the height of the land. Several voices cried out together: 'We are all on deck, sir.'

Then stillness again, with the great shadow gliding closer, towering higher, without light, without a sound. Such a hush had fallen on the ship that she might have been a bark of the dead floating in slowly under the very gate of Erebus.

'My God! Where are we?'

It was the mate moaning at my elbow. He was thunderstruck, and as it were deprived of the moral support of his whiskers. He clapped his hands and absolutely cried out, 'Lost!'

'Be quiet,' I said, sternly.

He lowered his tone, but I saw the shadowy gesture of his despair. 'What are we doing here?'

'Looking for the land wind.'

He made as if to tear his hair, and addressed me recklessly.

'She will never get out. You have done it, sir. I knew it'd end in something like this. She will never weather, and you are too close now to stay. She'll drift ashore before she's round. O my God!'

I caught his arm as he was raising it to batter his poor devoted head, and shook it violently.

'She's ashore already,' he wailed, trying to tear himself away.

'Is she? . . . Keep good full there!'

'Good full, sir,' cried the helmsman in a frightened, thin, childlike voice.

I hadn't let go the mate's arm and went on shaking it. 'Ready about, do you hear? You go forward'—shake—'and stop there'—shake—'and hold your noise'—shake—'and see these head-sheets properly overhauled'—shake, shake—shake.

And all the time I dared not look towards the land lest my heart should fail me. I released my grip at last and he ran forward as if fleeing for dear life.

I wondered what my double there in the sail-locker thought of this commotion. He was able to hear everything—and perhaps he was able to understand why, on my conscience, it had to be thus close—no less. My first order 'Hard alee!' re-echoed ominously under the towering shadow of Koh-ring as if I had shouted in a mountain gorge. And then I watched the land intently. In that smooth water and light wind it was impossible to feel the ship coming-to. No! I could not feel her. And my second self was making now ready to slip out and lower himself overboard. Perhaps he was gone already . . . ?

The great black mass brooding over our very mastheads began to pivot away from the ship's side silently. And now I forgot the secret stranger ready to depart, and remembered only that I was a total stranger to the ship. I did not know her. Would she do it? How was she to be handled?

I swung the mainyard and waited helplessly. She was perhaps stopped, and her very fate hung in the balance, with the black mass of Koh-ring like the gate of the everlasting night towering over her taff-rail. What would she do now? Had she way on her yet? I stepped to the side swiftly, and on the shadowy water I could see nothing except a faint phosphor-escent flash revealing the glassy smoothness of the sleeping surface. It was impossible to tell—and I had not learned yet the feel of my ship. Was she moving? What I needed was something easily seen, a piece of paper, which I could throw overboard and watch. I had nothing on me. To run down for it I didn't dare. There was no time. All at once my strained, yearning stare distinguished a white object floating within a yard of the ship's side. White on the black water. A phosphorescent flash passed under it. What was that thing? . . . I recognized my own floppy hat. It must have fallen off his head . . . and he didn't bother. Now I had what I wanted—the saving mark for my eyes. But I hardly thought of my other self, now gone from the ship, to be hidden for ever from all friendly faces, to be a fugitive and a vagabond on the earth, with no brand of the curse on his sane fore-head to stay a slaying hand . . . too proud to explain.

And I watched the hat—the expression of my sudden pity for his mere flesh. It had been meant to save his homeless head from the dangers of the sun. And now—behold—it was saving the ship, by serving me for a mark to help out the ignorance of my strangeness. Ha! It was drifting forward, warning me just in time that the ship had gathered sternway.

'Shift the helm,' I said in a low voice to the seaman standing still like a statue.

The man's eyes glistened wildly in the binnacle light as he jumped round to the other side and spun round the wheel.

I walked to the break of the poop. On the over-shadowed deck all hands stood by the forebraces waiting for my order. The stars ahead seemed to be gliding from right to left. And all was so still in the world that I heard the quiet remark 'She's round,' passed in a tone of intense relief between two seamen.

'Let go and haul.'

The foreyards ran round with a great noise, amidst cheery cries. And now the frightful whiskers made themselves heard giving various orders. Already the ship was drawing ahead. And I was alone with her. Nothing! no one in the world should stand now between us, throwing a shadow on the way of silent knowledge and mute affection, the perfect communion of a seaman with his first command.

Walking to the taffrail, I was in time to make out, on the very edge of a darkness thrown by a towering black mass like the very gateway of Erebus—yes, I was in time to catch an evanescent glimpse of my white hat left behind to mark the spot where the secret sharer of my cabin and of my thoughts, as though he were my second self, had lowered himself into the water to take his punishment: a free man, a proud swimmer striking out for a new destiny.

JACK LONDON

Make Westing

Whatever you do, make westing! make westing!
— Sailing directions for Cape Horn.

For seven weeks the *Mary Rogers* had been between
50° south in the Atlantic and 50° south in the
Pacific, which meant that for seven weeks she had
been struggling to round Cape Horn. For seven
weeks she had been either in dirt or close to dirt save
once, and then, following upon six days of excessive
dirt, which she had ridden out under the shelter of
the redoubtable Terra Del Fuego coast, she had
almost gone ashore during a heavy swell in the dead
calm that had suddenly fallen. For seven weeks she
had wrestled with the Cape Horn graybeards, and in
return been buffeted and smashed by them. She was
a wooden ship, and her ceaseless straining had
opened her seams, so that twice a day the watch
took its turn at the pumps.

The *Mary Rogers* was strained, the crew was
strained, and big Dan Cullen, master, was likewise
strained. Perhaps he was strained most of all, for
upon him rested the responsibility of that titanic

struggle. He slept most of the time in his clothes, though he rarely slept. He haunted the deck at night, a great, burly, robust ghost, black with the sunburn of thirty years of sea and hairy as an orangutan. He, in turn, was haunted by one thought of action, a sailing direction for the Horn: *Whatever you do, make westing! make westing!* It was an obsession. He thought of nothing else, except, at times, to blaspheme God for sending such bitter weather.

Make westing! He hugged the Horn, and a dozen times lay hove to with the iron Cape bearing east-by-north, or north-north-east, a score of miles away. And each time the eternal west wind smote him back and he made easting. He fought gale after gale, south to 64°, inside the antarctic drift ice, and pledged his immortal soul to the Powers of Darkness for a bit of westing, for a slant to take him around. And he made easting. In despair, he had tried to make the passage through the Straits of Le Maire. Halfway through, the wind hauled to the north'ard of northwest, the glass dropped to 28.88, and he turned and ran before a gale of cyclonic fury, missing, by a hairbreadth, piling up the *Mary Rogers* on the black-toothed rocks. Twice he had made west to the Diego Ramirez Rocks, one of the times saved between two snow squalls by sighting the gravestones of ships a quarter of a mile dead ahead.

Blow! Captain Dan Cullen instanced all his thirty years at sea to prove that never had it blown so before. The *Mary Rogers* was hove to at the time he gave the evidence, and to clinch it inside half an hour the *Mary Rogers* was hove down to the hatches. Her new maintopsail and brand new spencer were blown away like tissue paper; and five sails, furled and fast under double gaskets, were blown loose and stripped from the yards. And before morning the *Mary Rogers* was hove down twice again, and holes were knocked in her bulwarks to ease her decks from the weight of ocean that pressed her down.

On an average of once a week Captain Dan Cullen caught glimpses of the sun. Once, for ten minutes, the sun shone at midday, and ten minutes afterward a new gale was piping up, both watches were shortening sail, and all was buried in the obscurity of a driving snow squall. For a fortnight, once, Captain Dan Cullen was without a meridian or a chronometer sight. Rarely did he know his position within half of a degree, except when in sight of land; for sun and stars remained hidden behind the sky, and it was so gloomy that even at the best the horizons were poor for accurate observations. A gray gloom shrouded the world. The clouds were gray; the great driving seas were leaden gray; the smoking crests were a gray churning; even the occasional albatrosses were gray, while the snow flurries were not white, but gray under the somber pall of the heavens.

Life on board the *Mary Rogers* was gray—gray and gloomy. The faces of the sailors were blue-gray; they were afflicted with sea-cuts and sea boils and suffered exquisitely. They were shadows of men. For seven weeks, in the forecastle or on deck, they had not known what it was to be dry. They had forgotten what it was to sleep out a watch, and all watches it was, "All hands on deck!" They caught snatches of agonized sleep, and they slept in their oilskins ready for the everlasting call. So weak and worn were they that it took both watches to do the work of one. That was why both watches were on deck so much of the time. And no shadow of a man could shirk duty. Nothing less than a broken leg could enable a man to knock off work; and there were two such, who had been mauled and pulped by the seas that broke aboard.

One other man who was the shadow of a man was George Dorety. He was the only passenger on board, a friend of the firm, and he had elected to make the voyage for his health. But seven weeks of Cape Horn had not bettered his health. He gasped and panted in his bunk through the long, heaving nights; and when on deck he was so bundled up for warmth that he resembled a peripatetic old-clothes shop. At midday, eating at the cabin table in a gloom so deep that the swinging sea lamps burned always, he looked as blue-gray as the sickest, saddest man for'ard. Nor did gazing across the table at Captain Dan Cullen have any cheering effect upon him. Captain Cullen chewed and scowled and kept silent. The scowls were for God, and with every chew he reiterated the sole thought of his existence, which was *make westing*. He was a big hairy brute, and the sight of him was not stimulating to the other's appetite. He looked upon George Dorety as a Jonah, and told him so, once each meal, savagely transferring the scowl from God to the passenger and back again.

Nor did the mate prove a first aid to a languid appetite. Joshua Higgins by name, a seaman by profession and pull but a pot-walloper by capacity, he was a loose-jointed, sniffling creature, heartless and selfish and cowardly, without a soul, in fear of his life of Dan Cullen, and a bully over the sailors, who knew that behind the mate was Captain Cullen, the lawgiver and compeller, the driver and the destroyer, the incarnation of a dozen bucko mates. In that wild weather at the southern end of the earth, Joshua Higgins ceased washing. His grimy face usually robbed George Dorety of what little appetite he managed to accumulate. Ordinarily this lavatorial dereliction would have caught Captain Cullen's eye and vocabulary, but in the present his mind was filled with making westing, to the exclusion of all other things not contributory thereto. Whether the mate's face was clean or dirty had no bearing upon westing. Later on, when 50° south in the Pacific had been reached, Joshua Higgins would wash his face very abruptly. In the meantime, at the cabin table, where gray twilight alternated with lamplight while the lamps were being filled, George Dorety sat between the two men, one a tiger and the other a hyena, and wondered why God had made them. The second mate, Matthew Turner, was a true sailor and a man, but George Dorety did not have the solace of his company, for he ate by himself, solitary, when they had finished.

On Saturday morning, July 24, George Dorety awoke to a feeling of life and headlong movement. On deck he found the *Mary Rogers* running off before a howling southeaster. Nothing was set but the lower topsails and the foresail. It was all she could stand, yet she was making fourteen knots, as Mr. Turner shouted in Dorety's ear when he came on deck. And it was all westing. She was going around the Horn at last . . . if the wind held. Mr. Turner looked happy. The end of the struggle was in sight. But Captain Cullen did not look happy. He scowled at Dorety in passing. Captain Cullen did not want God to know that he was pleased with that wind. He had a conception of a malicious God, and believed in his secret soul that if God knew it was a desirable wind, God would promptly efface it and send a snorter from the west. So he walked softly before God, smothering his joy down under scowls and muttered curses, and so fooling God, for God was the only thing in the universe of which Dan Cullen was afraid.

All Saturday and Saturday night the *Mary Rogers* raced her westing. Persistently she logged her fourteen knots, so that by Sunday morning she had covered three hundred and fifty miles. If the wind held, she would make around. If it failed, and the snorter came from anywhere between southwest and north, back the *Mary Rogers* would be hurled and be no better off than she had been seven weeks before. And on Sunday morning the wind *was* failing. The big sea was going down and running smooth. Both watches were on deck setting sail after sail as fast as the ship could stand it. And now Captain Cullen went around brazenly before God, smoking a big cigar, smiling jubilantly, as if the failing wind delighted him, while down underneath he was raging against God for taking the life out of the blessed wind. *Make westing!* So he would, if God would only leave him alone. Secretly, he pledged himself anew to the Powers of Darkness, if they would let him make westing. He pledged himself so easily because he did not believe in the Powers of Darkness. He really believed only in God, though he did not know it. And in his inverted theology God was really the Prince of Darkness. Captain Cullen was a devil-worshiper, but he called the devil by another name, that was all.

At midday, after calling eight bells, Captain Cullen ordered the royals on. The men went aloft faster than they had gone in weeks. Not alone were they nimble because of the westing, but a benignant sun was shining down and limbering their stiff bodies. George Dorety stood aft, near Captain Cullen, less bundled in clothes than usual, soaking in the grateful warmth as he watched the scene. Swiftly and abruptly the incident occurred. There was a cry from the foreroyal yard of "Man overboard!" Somebody threw a life buoy over the side, and at the same instant the second mate's voice came aft, ringing and peremptory: "Hard down your helm!"

The man at the wheel never moved a spoke. He knew better, for Captain Dan Cullen was standing alongside of him. He wanted to move a spoke, to move all the spokes, to grind the wheel down, hard down, for his comrade drowning in the sea. He glanced at Captain Dan Cullen, and Captain Dan Cullen gave no sign.

"Down! Hard down!" the second mate roared, as he sprang aft.

But he ceased springing and commanding, and stood still, when he saw Dan Cullen by the wheel. And big Dan Cullen puffed at his cigar and said nothing. Astern, and going astern fast, could be seen the sailor. He had caught the life buoy and was clinging to it. Nobody spoke. Nobody moved. The men aloft clung to the royal yards and watched with terror-stricken faces. And the *Mary Rogers* raced on, making her westing. A long, silent minute passed.

"Who was it?" Captain Cullen demanded.

"Mops, sir," eagerly answered the sailor at the wheel.

Mops topped a wave astern and disappeared temporarily in the trough. It was a large wave, but it was no graybeard. A small boat could live easily in such a sea, and in such a sea the *Mary Rogers* could easily come to. But she could not come to and make westing at the same time.

For the first time in all his years, George Dorety was seeing a real drama of life and death—a sordid little drama in which the scales balanced an unknown sailor named Mops against a few miles of longitude. At first he had watched the man astern, but now he watched big Dan Cullen, hairy and black, vested with power of life and death, smoking a cigar.

Captain Dan Cullen smoked another long, silent minute. Then he removed the cigar from his mouth. He glanced aloft at the spars of the *Mary Rogers*, and overside at the sea.

"Sheet home the royals!" he cried.

Fifteen minutes later they sat at table, in the cabin, with food served before them. On one side of George Dorety sat Dan Cullen, the tiger, on the other side, Joshua Higgins, the hyena. Nobody spoke. On deck the men were sheeting home the skysails. George Dorety could hear their cries, while a persistent vision haunted him of a man called Mops, alive and well, clinging to a life buoy miles astern in that lonely ocean. He glanced at Captain Cullen, and experienced a feeling of nausea, for the man was eating his food with relish, almost bolting it.

"Captain Cullen," Dorety said, "you are in command of this ship, and it is not proper for me to comment now upon what you do. But I wish to say one thing. There is a hereafter, and yours will be a hot one."

Captain Cullen did not even scowl. In his voice

was regret as he said. "It was blowing a living gale. It was impossible to save the man."

"He fell from the royal yard," Dorety cried hotly. "You were setting the royals at the time. Fifteen minutes afterward you were setting the skysails."

"It was a living gale, wasn't it, Mr. Higgins?" Captain Cullen said, turning to the mate.

"If you'd brought her to, it'd have taken the sticks out of her," was the mate's answer. "You did the proper thing. Captain Cullen. The man hadn't a ghost of a show."

George Dorety made no answer, and to the meal's end no one spoke. After that, Dorety had his meals served in his stateroom. Captain Cullen scowled at him no longer, though no speech was exchanged between them, while the *Mary Rogers* sped north toward warmer latitudes. At the end of the week, Dan Cullen cornered Dorety on deck.

"What are you going to do when we get to 'Frisco?" he demanded bluntly.

"I am going to swear out a warrant for your arrest," Dorety answered quietly. "I am going to charge you with murder, and I am going to see you hanged for it."

"You're almighty sure of yourself," Captain Cullen sneered, turning on his heel.

A second week passed, and one morning found

George Dorety standing in the coach house companionway at the for'ard end of the long poop, taking his first gaze around the deck. The *Mary Rogers* was reaching full-and-by, in a stiff breeze. Every sail was set and drawing, including the staysails. Captain Cullen strolled for'ard along the poop. He strolled carelessly, glancing at the passenger out of the corner of his eye. Dorety was looking the other way, standing with head and shoulders outside the companionway, and only the back of his head was to be seen. Captain Cullen, with swift eye, embraced the main-staysail block and the head and estimated the distance. He glanced about him. Nobody was looking. Aft, Joshua Higgins, pacing up and down, had just turned his back and was going the other way. Captain Cullen bent over suddenly and cast the staysail sheet off from its pin. The heavy block hurtled through the air, smashing Dorety's head like an eggshell and hunting on and back and forth as the staysail whipped and slatted in the wind. Joshua Higgins turned around to see what had carried away, and met the full blast of the vilest portion of Captain Cullen's profanity.

"I made the sheet fast myself," whimpered the mate in the first lull, "with an extra turn to make sure. I remember it distinctly."

"Made fast?" the Captain snarled back, for the

benefit of the watch as it struggled to capture the flying sail before it tore to ribbons. "You couldn't make your grandmother fast, you useless hell's scullion. If you made that sheet fast with an extra turn, why in hell didn't it stay fast? That's what I want to know. Why in hell didn't it stay fast?"

The mate whined inarticulately.

"Oh, shut up!" was the final word of Captain Cullen.

Half an hour later he was as surprised as any when the body of George Dorety was found inside the companionway on the floor. In the afternoon, alone in his room, he doctored up the log.

"Ordinary seaman, Karl Brun," he wrote, "lost overboard from foreroyal yard in a gale of wind. Was running at the time, and for the safety of the ship did not dare come up to the wind. Nor could a boat have lived in the sea that was running."

On another page, he wrote:

"Had often warned Mr. Dorety about the danger he ran because of his carelessness on deck. I told him, once, that some day he would get his head knocked off by a block. A carelessly fastened mainstaysail sheet was the cause of the accident, which was deeply to be regretted because Mr. Dorety was a favorite with all of us."

Captain Dan Cullen read over his literary effort with admiration, blotted the page, and closed the log. He lighted a cigar and stared before him. He felt the *Mary Rogers* lift, and heel, and surge along, and knew that she was making nine knots. A smile of satisfaction slowly dawned on his black and hairy face. Well, anyway, he had made his westing and fooled God.

George A. Birmingham

The Mermaid

We were on our way home from Inishmore, where we had spent two days; Peter O'Flaherty among his relatives—for everyone on the island was kin to him—I among friends who give me a warm welcome when I go to them. The island lies some seventeen miles from the coast. We started on our homeward sail with a fresh westerly wind. Shortly after midday it backed round to the north and grew lighter. At five o'clock we were stealing along very gently through calm water with our mainsail boomed out against the shroud. The jib and foresail were drooping in limp folds. An hour later the mainsheet was hanging in the water and the boat drifted with the tide. Peter, crouching in the fore part of the cockpit, hissed through his clenched teeth, which is the way in which he whistles for a wind. He glanced all round the horizon, searching for signs of a breeze. His eyes rested finally on the sun, which lay low among some light, fleecy clouds. He gave it as his opinion that when it reached the point of setting it "might draw a light air after it from the eastward." For that it appeared we were to wait. I shrank from toil with the heavy sweeps. So, I am sure, did Peter, who is a good man in a boat, but averse from unnecessary labour. And there was really no need to row. The tide was carrying us homeward, and our position was pleasant enough. Save for the occasional drag of a block against the horse we had achieved unbroken silence and almost perfect peace.

We drifted slowly past Carrigeen Glos, a low sullen line of rocks. A group of cormorants, either gorged with mackerel fry or hopeless of an evening meal, perched together at one end of the reef, and stared at the setting sun. A few terns swept round and round overhead, soaring or sliding downwards with easy motion. A large seal lay basking on a bare rock just above the water's edge. I pointed it out to Peter, and he said it was a pity I had not got my rifle with me. I did not agree with him. If I had brought the rifle, Peter would have insisted on my shooting at the seal. I should certainly not have hit it on purpose, for I am averse from injuring gentle creatures; but I might perhaps have killed or wounded it by accident, for my shooting is very uncertain. In any case, I should have broken nature's peace, and made a horrible commotion. Perhaps the seal heard Peter's remark, or divined his feeling of hostility. It flopped across the rock and slid gracefully into the sea. We saw it afterwards swimming near the boat, looking at us with its curiously human, tender eyes.

"A man might mistake it for a mermaid," I said.

"He'd be a fool altogether that would do the like," said Peter.

He was scornful; but the seal's eyes were human. They made me think of mermaids.

"Them ones," said Peter, "is entirely different from seals. You might see a seal any day in fine weather. They're plenty. But the other ones——But sure you wouldn't care to be hearing about them."

"I've heard plenty about them," I said, "but it was all poetry and nonsense. You know well enough, Peter, that there's no such thing as a mermaid."

Peter filled his pipe slowly and lit it. I could see by the way he puffed at it that he was full of pity and contempt for my scepticism.

"Come now," I said, "did you ever see a mermaid?"

"I did not," said Peter, "but my mother was acquainted with one. That was in Inishmore, where I was born and reared."

I waited. The best chance of getting Peter to tell an interesting story is to wait patiently. Any attempt to goad him on by asking questions is like striking before a fish is hooked. The chance of getting either story or fish is spoiled.

"There was a young fellow in the island them times," said Peter, "called Anthony O'Flaherty. A kind of uncle of my father's he was, and a very fine man. There wasn't his equal at running or lepping, and they say he was terrible daring on the sea. That was before my mother was born, but she heard tell of what he did. When she knew him he was like an old man, and the heart was gone out of him."

At this point Peter stopped. His pipe had gone out. He relit it with immense deliberation. I made a mistake. By way of keeping the conversation going I asked a question.

"Did he see a mermaid?"

"He did," said Peter, "and what's more, he married one."

There Peter stopped again abruptly, but with an air of finality. He had, so I gathered, told me all he was going to tell me about the mermaid. I had blundered badly in asking my question. I suppose that some note of unsympathetic scepticism in my tone suggested to Peter that I was inclined to laugh at him. I did my best to retrieve my position. I sat quite silent and stared at the peak of the mainsail. The block on the horse rattled occasionally. The sun's rim touched the horizon. At last Peter was reassured and began again.

"It was my mother told me about it, and she

knew, for many's the time she did be playing with the young lads, her being no more than a little girleen at the time. Seven of them there was, and the second eldest was the one age with my mother. That was after herself left him."

"Herself" was vague enough; but I did not venture to ask another question. I took my eyes off the peak of the mainsail and fixed them inquiringly on Peter. It was as near as I dared go to asking a question.

"Herself," said Peter, "was one of them ones."

He nodded sideways over the gunwale of the boat. The sea, though still calm, was beginning to be moved by that queer restlessness which comes on it at sunset. The tide eddied in mysteriously oily swirls. The rocks to the eastward of us had grown dim. A gull flew by overhead, uttering wailing cries. The graceful terns had disappeared. A cormorant, flying so low that its wing-tips broke the water, sped across our bows to some far resting-place. I fell into a mood of real sympathy with stories about mermaids. I think Peter felt the change which had come over me.

"Anthony O'Flaherty," said Peter, "was a young man when he saw them first. It was in the little bay back west of the island, and my mother never rightly knew what he was doing there in the middle of the night; but there he was. It was the bottom of a low spring tide, and there's rocks off the end of the bay that's uncovered at the ebb of the springs. You've maybe seen them."

I have seen them, and Peter knew it well. I have seen more of them than I want to. There was an occasion when Peter and I lay at anchor in that bay, and a sudden shift of wind set us to beating out at three o'clock in the morning. The rocks were not uncovered then, but the waves were breaking fiercely over them. We had little room for tacking, and I am not likely to forget the time we went about a few yards to windward of them. The stretch of wild surf under our lee looked ghastly white in the dim twilight of the dawn. Peter knew what I was thinking.

"It was calm enough that night Anthony O'Flaherty was here," he said, "and there was a moon shining, pretty near a full moon, so Anthony could see plain. Well, there was three of them in it, and they playing themselves."

"Mermaids?"

This time my voice expressed full sympathy. The sea all round us was rising in queer round little waves, though there was no wind. The boom snatched at the blocks as the boat rocked. The sail was ghostly white. The vision of a mermaid would not have surprised me greatly.

"The beautifullest ever was seen," said Peter,

"with neither shift nor shirt on them, only just themselves, and the long hair of them. Straight it was and black, only for a taste of green in it. You wouldn't be making a mistake between the like of them and seals, not if you'd seen them right the way Anthony O'Flaherty did."

Peter made this reflection a little bitterly. I was afraid the recollection of my unfortunate remark about seals might have stopped him telling the story, but it did not.

"Once Anthony had seen them," he said, "he couldn't rest content without he'd be going to see them again. Many a night he went and saw neither sight nor light of them, for it was only at spring tides that they'd be there, on account of the rocks not being uncovered any other time. But at the bottom of the low springs they were there right enough, and sometimes they'd be swimming in the sea and sometimes they'd be sitting on the rocks. It was wonderful the songs they'd sing—like the sound of the sea set to music was what my mother told me, and she was told by them that knew. The people did be wondering what had come over Anthony, for he was different like from what he had been, and nobody knew what took him out of his house in the middle of the night at the spring tides. There was a girl that they had laid down for him to marry, and Anthony bad no objection to her before he had seen them ones; but after he had seen them he wouldn't look at the girl. She had a middling good fortune, too, but sure he didn't care about that."

I could understand Anthony's feelings. The air of wind which Peter had promised, drawn from its cave by the lure of the departing sun, was filling our head-sails. I hauled in the mainsheet gently, hand over hand, and belayed it. The boat slipped along close-hauled. The long line of islands which guards the entrance of our bay lay dim before us. Over the shoulder of one of them I could see the lighthouse, still a distinguishable patch of white against the looming grey of the land. The water rippled mournfully under our bows and a long pale wake stretched astern from our counter. "Fortune," banked money, good heifers and even enduringly fruitful fields seemed very little matters to me then. They must have seemed still less, far less, to Anthony O'Flaherty after he had seen those white sea-maidens with their green-black hair.

"There was a woman on the island in those times," said Peter, "a very aged woman, and she had a kind of plaster she made which cured the cancer, drawing it out by the roots, and she could tell what was good for the chin cough, and the women did like to have her with them when their children was born, she being knowledgeable in them matters. I'm told the priests didn't like her, for there were things she knew which it mightn't be right that anyone would know, things that's better left to the clergy. Whether she guessed what was the matter with Anthony, or whether he up and told her straight, my mother never knew. It could be that he told her, for many a one used to go to her for a charm when the butter wouldn't come, or a cow, maybe, was pining; so it wouldn't surprise me if Anthony went to her."

Peter crept aft. He took a pull on the jib-sheet and belayed it again; but I do not believe that he really cared much about the set of the sail. That was his excuse. He wanted to be nearer to me. There is something in stories like this, told in dim twilight, with dark waters sighing near at hand, which makes men feel the need of close human companionship. Peter seated himself on the floor-boards at my feet, and I felt a certain comfort in the touch of his arm on my leg.

"Well," he went on, "according to the old hag—and what she said was true enough, however she learnt it—them ones doesn't go naked all the time, but only when they're playing themselves on the rocks at low tide, the way Anthony seen them. Mostly, they have a kind of cloak that they wear, and they take the same cloaks off of them when they're up above the water and lay them down on the rocks. If so be that a man could put his hand on e'er a cloak, the one that owned it would have to follow him, whether she wanted to or not. If it was to the end of the world she'd have to follow him, or to Spain, or to America, or wherever he might go. And what's more, she'd have to do what he bid her, be the same good or bad, and be with him if he wanted her, so long as he kept the cloak from her. That's what the old woman told Anthony, and she was a skilful woman, well knowing the nature of beasts and men, and of them that's neither beasts nor men. You'll believe me now that Anthony wasn't altogether the same as other men when I tell you that he laid his mind down to get his hand down on one of the cloaks. He was a good swimmer, so he was, which is what few men on the island can do, and he knew that he'd be able to fetch out to the rock where them ones played themselves."

I was quite prepared to believe that Anthony was inspired by a passion far out of the common. I know nothing more terrifying than the chill embrace of the sea at night-time. To strike out through the slimy weeds which lie close along the surface at the ebb point of a spring tide, to clamber on low rocks, half-awash for an hour or two at midnight, these are things I could not willingly do.

"The first time he went for to try it," said Peter, "he felt a bit queer in himself, and he thought it would do him no harm if he was to bless himself. So he did, just as he was stepping off the shore into the water. Well, it might as well have been a shot he fired, for the minute he did it they were off and their cloaks along with them; and Anthony was left there. It was the sign of the cross had them frightened, for that same is what they can't stand, not having souls that religion would be any use to. It was the old woman told Anthony that after, and you'd think it would have been a warning to him not to make or meddle with the like of them any more. But it only made him the more determined. He went about without speaking to man or woman, and if anybody spoke to him he'd curse terrible, till the time of the next spring tide. Then he was off to the bay again, and sure enough them ones was there. The water was middling rough that night, but it didn't daunt Anthony. It pleased him, for he thought he'd have a better chance of getting to the rocks without them taking notice of him if there was some noise loud enough to drown the noise he'd be making himself. So he crept out to the point of the cliff on the south side of the bay, which is as near as he could get to the rocks. You remember that?"

I did. On the night when we beat out of the bay

against a rising westerly wind we went about once under the shadow of the cliff, and almost before we had full way on the boat, stayed her again beside the rocks. Anthony's swim, though terrifying, was short.

"That time he neither blessed himself nor said a prayer, but slipped into the water, and off with him, swimming with all his strength. They didn't see him, for they were too busy with their playing to take much notice, and of course, they couldn't be expecting a man to be there. Without Anthony had shouted they wouldn't have heard him, for the sea was loud on the rocks and their own singing was louder. So Anthony got there and he crept up on the rocks behind them, and the first thing his hand touched was one of the cloaks. He didn't know which of them it belonged to, and he didn't care. It wasn't any one of the three in particular he wanted, for they were all much about the same to look at, only finer than any woman ever was seen. So he rolled the cloak round his neck, the way he'd have his arms free for swimming, and back with him into the water, heading for shore as fast as he was able."

"And she followed him?" I asked.

"She did so. From that day till the day she left him she followed him, and she did what she was bid, only for one thing. She wouldn't go to Mass, and when the chapel bell rang she'd hide herself. The sound of it was what she couldn't bear. The people thought that queer and there was a great deal of talk about it in the island, some saying she must be Protestant, and more thinking that she might be something else. But no one had a word to say against her any way. She was a good housekeeper, washing, making and mending for Anthony, and minding the children. Seven of them there was, and all boys."

The easterly breeze freshened as the night fell. I could see the great eye of the lighthouse blinking at me on the weather side of the boat. It became necessary to go about, but I gave the order to Peter very reluctantly. He handled the head-sheets, and then, instead of settling down in his old place, leaned his elbows on the coaming and stared into the sea. I felt that I must run the risk of asking him a question.

"What happened in the end?" I asked.

"The end, is it? Well, in the latter end she left him. But there was things before that. Whether it was the way the priests talked to him about her— there was a priest in it them times that was too fond of interfering, and that's what some of them are—or whether there was goings-on within in the inside of the house that nobody knew anything about—and there might have been, for you couldn't tell what one of them ones might do or mightn't. Whatever way it was, Anthony took to drinking more than he ought. There was poteen made on the island then, and whisky was easy come by if a man wanted it, and Anthony took too much of it."

Peter paused and then passed judgment, charitably, on Anthony's conduct. "I wouldn't be too hard on a man for taking a drop an odd time."

I was glad to hear Peter say that. I myself had found it necessary from time to time, for the sake of an old friendship, not to be too hard on Peter.

"Nobody would have blamed him," Peter went on, "if he had behaved himself when he had a drop taken; but that's what he didn't seem able to do. He beat her. Sore and heavy he beat her, and that's what no woman, whether she was a natural woman or one of the other kind, could be expected to put up with. Not that she said a word. She didn't. Nor nobody would have known he beat her if he hadn't taken to beating the young lads along with her. It was them that told what was going on. But there wasn't one on the island would interfere. The people did be wondering that she didn't put the fear of God into Anthony, but of course that's what she couldn't do on account of his having the cloak hid away from her. So long as he had that she was bound to put up with whatever he did. But it wasn't forever.

"The house was going to rack and ruin with the way Anthony wouldn't mind it on account of his being three parts drunk most of the time. At last rain was coming through the roof. When Anthony saw that he came to himself a bit and sent for my grandfather and settled with him to put a few patches of new thatch on the worst places. My grandfather was the best man at thatching that there was in the island in them days, and he took the job though he misdoubted whether he'd ever be paid for it. Anthony never came next or nigh him when he was working, which shows that he hadn't got his senses rightly. If he had he'd have kept an eye on what my grandfather was doing, knowing what he knew, though of course my grandfather didn't know. Well, one day, my grandfather was dragging off the old thatch near the chimney. It was middling late in the evening, as it might be six or seven o'clock, and he was thinking of stopping his work when all of a sudden he came on what he thought might be an old petticoat bundled away in the thatch. It was red, he said, but when he put his hand on it he knew it wasn't flannel, nor it wasn't cloth, nor it wasn't like anything he'd ever felt before in his life. There was a hole in the roof where my grandfather had the roof stripped, and he could see down into the kitchen. Anthony's wife was there with the youngest of the boys in her arms. My grandfather was as much in dread of her as any other one, but he thought it would be no more than civil to tell her what he'd found.

"Begging your pardon, ma'am," he said, "but I'm after finding what maybe belongs to you hid away in the thatch."

"With that he threw down the red cloak he had in his hand. She didn't speak a word, but she laid down the baby out of her arms and she walked out of the house. That was the last my mother seen of her. And that was the last anyone seen of her on the island, unless maybe Anthony. Nobody knows what he saw. He stopped off the drink from that day; but it wasn't much use his stopping it. He used to go round at spring tides to the bay where he had seen her first. He did that five times, or maybe six. After that he took to his bed and died. It could be that his heart was broke."

We slipped past the point of the pier. Peter crept forward and crouched on the deck in front of the mast. I peered into the gloom to catch sight of our mooring-buoy.

"Let her away a bit yet," said Peter. "Now luff her, luff her all you can."

The boat edged up into the wind. Peter, flat on his stomach, grasped the buoy and hauled it on board. The fore-sheets beat their tattoo on the deck. The boom swung sharply across the boat.

Ten minutes later we were leaning together across the boom gathering in the mainsail.

"What became of the boys?" I asked.

"Is it Anthony O'Flaherty's boys? The last of them went to America twenty years ago. But sure that was before you came to these parts."

The Captain's Arm

Seafaring men knew it for a chief characteristic of Captain Price—his quiet, unresting watchfulness. Forty years of sun and brine had bunched the puckers at the corners of his eyes and hardened the lines of his big brown face; but the outstanding thing about him was still that silent wariness, as of a man who had warning of something impending. It went a little strangely with his figure of a massive, steel-and-hickory shipmaster, soaked to the soul with the routine of his calling. It seemed to give token of some faculty held in reserve, to hint at an inner life, as it were; and not a few of the frank and simple men who went to sea with him found it disconcerting. Captains who could handle a big steamship as a cyclist manages a bicycle they had seen before; they recognized in him the supreme skill, the salt-pickled nerve, the iron endurance of a proven sailor; but there their experience ended and the depths began.

Sooner or later, most of them went to the *Burdock*'s chief mate for an explanation of the unknown quality. "What makes your father act so?" was a common form of the question. Arthur Price would smile and shake his handsome head.

"It's not acting," he would say. "You drop off to sleep some night on this bridge, and you'll find out what he's after. He's after you if you don't keep your weather eye liftin'; and don't you forget it."

In those days the *Burdock* had a standing charter from Cardiff to Barcelona and back with ore to Swansea, a comfortable round trip which brought the captain and his son home for one week in every six. It suited the mate's convenience excellently, for he was a man of social habits, and he had at last succeeded in interesting Miss Minnie Davis in his movements. She was the daughter of the *Burdock*'s owner, and Arthur Price's cousin in some remote degree, a plump, clean, clever Welsh girl, of quick intelligence and pleasant good nature. He was a tall young man, a little leggy in his way, who filled the eye splendidly. Women said of him that he "looked every inch a sailor"; matrons who watched his progress with Minnie Davis considered that they would make a handsome couple. Captain Price, for all his watchfulness, saw nothing of the affair. He approved of Minnie, though; she was born to a share in that life in which ships are bread-winners, and never had to be shoo'd out of the way of hauling or hoisting gear when she came down aboard the *Burdock* in dock. Her way was straight across the deck to the poop ladder and for'ard to the chart-house along the fore-and-aft bridge, trim, quiet-footed, familiar. "What did you find in the Bay?" she would ask, as she shook hands with Captain Price; and he would answer as to one who understood: "It was piling up a bit from the sou'-west"; or "smooth enough to skate on, as the case might be. Then, without further formality, he would return to his papers, and Arthur Price would hand over his work to the third mate and wash his hands before coming up to make himself agreeable. He always had more to say about the trip than his father, and he was prone to translate the weather into shore speech. Minnie only half-liked his fashion of talking of "storms" and "tempests"; but there was plenty else in him she liked well enough. Best of all, perhaps, she liked the slight of him—a head taller than his father, clean-shaven and accurately groomed, smiling readily and moving easily; he was a capital picture.

She fell into a way of driving down to see the *Burdock* off. It was thus that Captain Price learned how matters stood. He came straight from the office to the ship, on a brisk July day, and went off to her at her buoys in the mud-pilot's boat. All was clear for a start and the lock was waiting; Arthur Price, in the gold-laced cap he used as due to his rank, was standing by to cast off. The captain went forthwith to the bridge; Minnie on the dock-head could see his black shore-hat over the weather-cloths and his white collar of ceremony. She smiled a little, for she did not know quite enough to see the art with which the Captain drew off from his moorings under his own steam, nor his splendid handling of the big boat as he bustled her down the crowded dock and laid her blunt nose cleanly between the piers of the lock. She was watching the brass-buttoned chief mate lording it on the fo'c'sle head, as he passed the lines to haul into the lock; Captain Price was watching him, too. He saw him smiling and talking over the rail to the girl.

"Slack off that spring," he roared suddenly, as they began to let the ship down to the sea level, and the mate jumped for the coil on the bitts.

"Keep your eyes about you, for'ard there," ordered the captain tersely.

"Aye, aye, sir," sang out the mate cheerfully.

The mud pilot, beside the captain on the bridge, grinned agreeably.

"Arthur's got an eye in his head, indeed," he remarked, and lifted his cap to Minnie.

The Captain snorted, and gave his whole attention to hauling out, only turning his head at the last minute to wave a farewell to his owner's daughter.

The mud-pilot took charge and brought her clear; and as soon as he had gone over to his boat, the captain rang for full steam ahead and waited for the mate to take the bridge.

The young man came up smiling. "It's a fine morning, Father," he remarked, as he walked over to the binnacle.

"Mister Mate," said the captain harshly; "you all but lost me that hawser."

"Just in time, wasn't I?" replied the mate pleasantly.

"I don't reckon to slack off and take in my lines myself," went on the Captain. "I reckon to leave that to my officers. And if an officer carries away a five-inch manila through makin' eyes at girls on the pier-head, I dock his wages for the cost of it, and I log him for neglectin' his duty."

The mate looked at him sharply for a moment; the captain scowled back:

"Have you got anything to say to me?" demanded the captain.

"Yes," said the mate, "I have." He broke into a smile. "But it's something I can't say while you're actin' the man-o'-war captain on your bridge. It doesn't concern the work o' the ship."

"What does it concern?" asked the captain.

"Me," said the mate. He folded his arms across

the binnacle and looked into his father's face confidently. The captain softened.

"Well, Arthur?" he said.

"That was Minnie on the pier-head," said the mate. The captain nodded. "I was up at their place last night," the young man continued, "and we had a talk—she and I—and so it came about that we fixed things between us. Mr. Dave, is agreeable, so long——"

"Hey, what's this?" The captain stared at his son amazedly. "What was it you fixed up with Minnie?"

"Why, to get married," replied the mate, reddening. "I was telling you. Her father's willing, as long as we wait till I get a command before we splice."

"*You* to marry Minnie!" The mate stiffened at the emphasis on the "you." The captain was fighting for expression "Why," he said, "why—why, you'd 'a' carried away that hawser if I hadn't sung out at ye."

"Father," said the mate. "Mr. Davis'll give me a ship"

"What ship?" demanded the captain.

"The first he can," replied the other. "He's thinkin' of buyin' the *Stormberg*, Wrench Wylie's big freighter, and he'd shift you on to her. Then I'd have the *Burdock*."

"Then you'd have the *Burdock*!" The captain leaned his elbow on the engine-room telegraph and faced his son. His expression was wholly compounded of perplexity and surprise. He let his eyes wander aft, along the big ship's trim perspective to the short poop, and forward to where her bluff bows sawed at the skyline.

"She's a fine old boat," he said at last, and stood up with a sigh. "But she needs watching."

The mate felt a thrill of relief. "I'll watch her," he said comfortably. "But don't you want to wish me luck, Father?"

"Not luck," said the captain; "not luck, my boy. You run her to a hair and keep your eyes slit and you won't want luck. Luck's a lubber's standby. But Minnie's a fine girl." He shook his head thoughtfully. "She'll rouse you up, maybe."

The mate laughed, and at the sound of it the captain frowned again.

"Now, lean off that binnacle," he said shortly. "I want to get the bearings."

It was not till an hour later that he went to his cabin to shed his shore-going gear for ordinary apparel; and as soon as this was done he reached down the register from the book-shelf over his bunk to look up the *Stormberg*.

"H'm," he growled, standing over the book at his desk. "Built in 1889 on the Clyde. *I* know her style. Five thousand tons, and touch the steam steering-gear if you dare! Blast her, and blast Davis for a junk-buying fool!"

He closed the book with a slam and glanced mechanically up at the tell-tale compass that hung over his bed.

"There's Arthur half a point off already," he said, and made for the bridge.

Arthur Price believed honestly that more was exacted from him than from other chief mates; and early in that passage he concluded that the Old Man was severer than ever. The *Burdock* butted into a summer gale before she was clear of the Bristol Channel, a free wind that came from the south-west driving a biggish sea before it. It was nothing to give real trouble, but Captain Price took charge in the dog watch and set the mate and his men to making all fast about decks. With his sou'wester flapped back from his forehead and his oilskin coat shrouding him to the heels, he leaned on the bridge rail, vociferous and imperative, and his harsh voice hunted the workers from one task to another. He had lashings on the anchors and fresh wedges to the battens of all hatches; the winches chocked off and covered over and new pins in the davit blocks. This took time, but when it was done he was not yet satisfied; the mate had to get out gear and rig a couple of preventer funnel stays. The men looked ahead at the weather and wondered what the skipper saw in it to make such a bother; the second and third mates winked at one another behind Arthur Price's back; and he, the chief mate, sulked.

"That's all, I suppose?" he asked the Captain when he got on the bridge again at last.

"No," was the sharp answer. "It's not all. Speak the engine-room and ask the chief how he's hitting it."

"All sweet," reported the mate as he hung up the speaking tube.

"That's right," said the captain. "You always want to know that, Mister Mate. And the lights?"

"All bright, sir," said the mate.

"Then you can go down and get something to eat," said the captain. "And see that the hand wheel's clear as you go."

It breezed up that night, and as the *Burdock* cleared the tail of Cornwall, the heavy Atlantic water came aboard. She was a sound ship, though, and Captain Price knew her as he knew the palms of his hands. Screened behind the high weather-cloths, he drove her into it, while the tall seas filled her forward main deck rail-deep and her bows pounded away in a mast-high smother of spray. From the binnacle amidships to the weather wing of the bridge was his dominion, while the watch officer straddled down to leeward; both with eye boring at the darkness ahead and on either beam, where there came and went the pin-point lights of ships.

Arthur Price relieved the bridge at midnight, but the captain held on.

"Ye see how she takes it?" he bawled down the wind to his son. "No excuse for steaming wide; ye can drive her to a hair. Keep your eyes on that light to port; we don't want anything bumping into us."

"You wouldn't ease her a bit, then?" shouted the mate, the wind snatching his words.

"Ease her!" was the reply. "You'd have her edging info France. She'll lie her course while we drive her."

When dawn came up the sea had mounted; the Bay was going to be true to its name. Captain Price went to his chart-house at midnight, to sleep on a settle; but by his orders the *Burdock* was kept to her course and her gait, battering away at the gale contentedly. After breakfast, he took another look round and then went below to rest in his bunk, while the tell-tale compass swam in wild eccentrics above his upturned face. After a while he dozed off to sleep, lulled by the click of furnishings that rendered to the ship's roll, the drum of the seas on her plates, and the swish of loose water across the deck.

He was roused by his steward. That menial laid a

hand on his shoulder and he was forthwith awake and competent.

"A ship to windward, sir, showin' flags," said the steward. "The mate 'ud be glad if you'd go to the bridge."

"A'right," said the captain, and stood up. "In distress, eh?"

"By the looks of her, sir," admitted the steward, who had been a waiter ashore. "She seems to be a mast or two short, sir, so far as I can tell. But I couldn't be sure."

He helped the captain into his oilskins deftly, pulling his jacket down under the long coat, and held the door open for him.

Some three miles to windward the stranger lay, an appealing vagabond. The captain found his son standing on the flag chest, braced against a stanchion, watching her through a pan of glasses, when she peeped up, a momentary silhouette, over the tall seas. He turned as the captain approached.

"Can't make out her flags, sir," he said. "Too much wind. Looks like a barque with only her mizen standing."

"Gimme the glass," said the captain, climbing up beside him. He braced himself against the irons and took a look at her, swinging accurately to the roll of the ship. Beneath him the wind-whipped water tumbled in grey leagues; the stranger seemed poised on the rim of it. From her gaff a dot of a flag showed a blur against the sky, and a string from her mast-head was equally vague.

"That'll be her ensign upside down at the gaff," he said. "Port your helm there; we'll go down and look at her."

"Aye, aye, sir." The mate passed the word and came over. "How would it be to see one of the boats clear, father?"

"Aren't the boats clear?" demanded the captain.

"Oh, yes, they're clear," replied the mate. "You had us put new pins in the blocks, you know." He met his father's steady eye defiantly. "When are a steamer's boats ever clear for hoisting out?" he asked.

"Always, when the mate's fit for his job," was the answer. "Go and make sure of the starboard lifeboat, and call the watch."

The captain took his ship round to windward of the distressed vessel, running astern of her within a quarter of a mile. She proved to be the remains of a barque, as the mate had guessed, a deep-laden wooden ship badly swept by the sea. From the wing of the bridge the Captain's glasses showed him the length of her deck, cluttered with the wreck of houses torn up by the roots, while the fall of the spars had taken her starboard bulwarks with it. Her boats were gone; a davit stuck up at the end of the poop crumpled like a ram's horn; and by the taffrail her worn and sodden crew clustered and cheered the *Burdock*.

The captain rang off his engines and rang again to stand by in the engine-room. The mate came up the ladder to him while his hand was yet at the telegraph.

"Lifeboat's all clear for lowering, sir," he said. "Noble, Peters, Hansen and Ryland are to go in her." He waited.

The old captain stood looking at the wreck, while the steamship rolled tumultuously in the trough.

"Who goes in charge?" he asked, after a minute's silence.

"I'll go, Father," said the mate eagerly. He paused, but the captain said nothing.

"You know," proceeded the mate, "Father, you *do* know there's none of 'em here can handle a boat like me."

"Aye," said the captain, "you can do it." He looked at his son keenly. "It 'ud make a good yarn to spin to Minnie," he said, with an unwilling smile.

The mate laughed agreeably. "Dear Minnie," he said. "Then I'll go, Father."

"And I'll just see to the hoisting out of that boat,"

said the captain. "Good thing I had you put in the new pins."

The third mate on the bridge rang for steam and made a lee for the lowering of the lifeboat, the hands put a strain on the tackles, and the carpenter and bo'sun went to work to knock out the chocks on which she rested. Her steel-shod keel had rusted into them.

"Hoist away on your forward tackle," ordered the captain. "Belay! Make fast! Now get a hold of this guy. Lively there, you men. Noble, aloft on the booms and shoulder her over."

She canted clear of the groove in the chocks as they swung the forward davit out and the captain stepped abaft the men who hauled.

"Lively now," he called. "Don't keep those chaps waiting, men. After davit tackle, haul! Up with her."

The bo'sun, stooping, looped the fall of the tackle into the snatch-block; the men, under the captain's eye, tumbled to and gave way, holding the weight gallantly as the rail swung down and putting their backs into the pull as she rolled back.

"Up with her!" shouted the captain, and she tore loose from her bed. "Vast hauling! Belay! Now out with the davit, men."

He stepped a pace forward as they passed out the line. "Haul away," he was saying, when the bo'sun shouted hoarsely and tried to reach him with a dash across the slippery deck planks. The mate screamed, the captain humped his shoulders for the blow. It all happened in a flash of disaster; the boat's weight pulled the pin from the cheeks of the block and down she came, her stern thudding thickly into the deck, while the captain, limp and senseless, rolled inertly to the scuppers.

When he came to he was in his bunk. He opened his eyes with a shiver upon the familiar cabin, with its atmosphere of compact neatness, its gleaming paint and bright-work. A throb of brutal pain in his head wrung a grunt from him, and then he realized that something was wrong with his right arm. He tried to move it, to bring it above the bedclothes to look at it, and the effort surprised an oath from him, and left him dizzy and shaking. The white jacket of the steward came through a mist that was about him.

"Better, I hope, sir," the steward was saying. "Beggin' your pardon, but you'd better lie still, sir. Is there anything I could bring you, sir?"

"Did the boat fall on me?" asked the captain, carefully. His voice seemed thin to himself.

"Not *on* you, sir," replied the steward. "Not so to speak, on top of you. The keel 'it you on the shoulder, sir, an' you contracted a thump on the 'ead."

"And the wreck?" asked the captain.

"The wreck's crew is aboard, sir; barque *Vavasour*, of London, sir. The mate brought 'em off most gallantly, sir. I was to tell 'im when you come to, sir."

"Tell him, then," said the captain, and closed his eyes wearily. The pain in his head blurred his thoughts, but his lifelong habit of waking from sleep to full consciousness, with no twilight of muddled faculties intervening, held good yet. He remembered, now, the new pins in the blocks, and there was even a tincture of amusement in his reflections. A soft tread beside him made him open his eyes.

"Well, Arthur," he said.

The tall young mate was beside him.

"Ah, Father," he said cheerfully. "Picking up a bit, eh? That's good. Ugly accident, that."

"Yes," replied the captain, looking up into his face. "Block split, I suppose?"

"Yes," said the mate. "That's it. How do you feel?"

"You didn't notice the block, I suppose, when you put the new pins in?" asked the captain.

"Can't say I did," answered the mate, "or I'd have changed it. You're not going to blame me surely, Father."

The captain smiled. "No, Arthur, I'm not going to blame you," he said. "I want to hear how you brought off that barque's crew. Is it a good yarn for Minnie?"

At Barcelona the captain went to hospital and they took off his right arm at the shoulder. The *Burdock* went back without him, and he lay in his bed wondering how it was that the loss of an arm should make a man feel lonely.

He was quickly about again. His body was clean from the bone out, clean and hard, and he had never been ill. When the time came to take a walk, he arrayed himself in shore-going black. It cost him an infinity of trouble and more than an hour of the morning to dress himself with one hand, but he would not have help. Then it was that he discovered a strange thing; it was his right arm, the arm that was gone, that hindered him. The scars of the amputation had healed, but unless he bore the fact deliberately in mind, he felt the arm to be there. He tried to button his braces with it, to knot his tie, to lace his boots, and had to overtake the impulse and correct it with an effort. When his clothes were on, he put his right hand in his trousers pocket, then remembered that it was not there, and withdrew hastily the hand he had not got. During the walk the same trouble remained with him; it muddled him when he bought tobacco and tried to pick up the change. Before he slept that night, he dropped on his knees at his bedside, and folded the left hand of flesh against the right hand of dreamstuff in prayer.

When his time came to go home in the *Burdock*, he was an altered man. The quiet, all-observant scrutiny had gone, and the officers who greeted him as he came up the accommodation ladder saw it at once. Arthur Price was now in command, a breezy, good-looking captain in blue serge and gold braid.

"You've got her, then, Arthur?" said the old man, as he reached the deck and stood looking about him.

"Yes, I've got her," answered his son. "That your kit, Father. Sewell (to the chief mate), send a couple of hands to get that dunnage aboard. Come along below, Father."

He tucked his arm into his father's and led him down. Mildly taking stock of the well-remembered surroundings, the old man noticed he was being taken to the captain's state-room, and an impulse of gratitude moved him. But he was glad he did not speak of it when his son put aside the curtains at the door for him, and he saw that this was not to be his room. New chintzes took the place of his old leather cushions; a big photograph of Minnie stood on the lid of the chronometer case, and the broken-backed Admiralty guides, ocean directories and the rest were reinforced by a brigade of smartly-bound novels.

"Sit down," said Arthur, "and make yourself at

home till they get your dunnage in. I've put you in the spare cabin in the port alleyway; you'll find it nice and quiet there. How are you feeling, Father? Would you care for a drink?"

"Yes, I'd like a tot," replied the old man. "Shall I ring for your steward?"

"Don't you trouble," said Arthur. "I've got it here." It was in the cupboard under the chronometer, a whole case of whisky. "I carry my own," explained the mate; "I don't approve of old Davis's taste in whisky. Help yourself, Father."

"How is Minnie?" asked the old man as he set down his glass.

"She's all right," was the reply. "I wanted to tell you about that. We go into dry dock when we get back from this trip, and Minnie and I'll get married before I take her out again. Quick work, isn't it?"

The old captain nodded; the young captain smiled.

"You'll be bringing Minnie out for the trip, I suppose?" asked the elder.

"That's my idea," agreed Arthur.

"You're a lucky chap," said the old man slowly. He hesitated. "You've got your ship in hand, eh, Arthur?"

"I've got her down to a fine point," said Arthur emphatically. "You needn't bother about me, Father.

I know my job, and I don't need more teaching. I wish you'd get to understand that. You know Davis has bought the *Stormberg*?"

"I didn't know," said the old man with a sigh. "It don't matter to me, anyhow. I'd be reaching for the engine telegraph with my right hand as like as not. No, Arthur, I've done. I'll bother young officers no more."

The run home was an easy one, but it confirmed old Captain Price in his resolution to have done with the sea. Two or three times he fell about decks; a small roll, the commonplace movement of a well-driven steamship in a seaway shook him from his balance, and that missing arm, which always seemed to be there, let him down. He would reach for a stanchion with it to steady himself, and none of his falls served to cure him of the persistent delusion that he was not a cripple. He tried to pick things up with it and let glasses and the like fall every day. The officers and engineers, men who had sailed with him at his ablest, saw his weakness quickly, and, with the ready tact that comes to efficient seafarers, never showed by increased deference or any sign that they were conscious of the change. It was only Arthur who went aside to make things easy for him, to cut his food for him at table, and so forth.

From Swansea he went home by train; Minnie

and her kindly old father met him and made much of him. Old Davis was a man who had built up his own fortune, scraping tonnage together bit by bit, from the time when, as a captain, he had salved a crazy derelict and had her turned over to him by the underwriters in quittance of his claims. Now he owned a little fleet of good steamships of respectable burthen, and was an esteemed owner. He did not press the *Stormberg* on Captain Price. The two old men understood each other.

"I don't want her," Captain Price told him. "There's a time for nursin' tender engines and a time for scrappin' them. I'm for the scrap heap, David. I'm not the man I was. I don't put faith in myself no more. It's Arthur's turn now."

David Davis nodded. "Yes, then. Well, well, now! It's a pity, too, John. But you know what's best, to be sure. I don't want you to go without a ship while I've got a bottom afloat, but I don't want you to put the *Stormberg* to roost on the rocks of Lundy neither. So you wouldn't put faith in yourself no more?"

"No," said Captain Price, frowning reflectively. "I wouldn't, and that's the truth." He was seated in a plush-covered arm-chair in Davis's parlour, and now he leaned forward. "It's this arm of mine. It isn't there, but I can't get rid of the feeling of it. I'm always reachin' for things with it. I'd be reachin' for the telegraph in a hurry, I make no doubt."

"That's funny," said Davis, in sympathy. "Well, then, you just stop visiting with me. I've no mind to be alone in the house when your Arthur's gone off with my Minnie. He'll push the *Burdock*, back an' fore for us, and we'll sit ashore like gentlemen. He makes a good figure of a skipper, don't he, John?"

Old Captain Price sighed. "Aye, he looks well on the bridge," he said. "I hope he'll watch the ship, though; she's a big old tub to handle."

He saw the *Burdock* into dry dock and strolled down each day to look at her. Minnie and Arthur were busy with preparations for the wedding. But the girl found time to go down once with the old man, and he took her into the dock under the steamship.

"A big thing she looks from here," he said, half to himself.

The girl looked forward. Over them the bottom plates of the *Burdock* made a great sloping roof; her rolling chocks stood out like galleries. Her lines bulged heavily out, and the girl saw the immensity of the great fabric, the power of the tool her husband should wield.

"She's big, indeed," she answered. "Five thousand tons and forty lives in one man's hands. It's splendid, Uncle. And Arthur," her voice softened pleasantly, "is the man."

The old captain wheeled on her sharply. "Tons and lives!" he cried. "Tons and lives be damned! It's not for them she's been run to a thumb-span and tended like a sick baby. It's for the clean honesty of it, to do a captain's work like a wise captain and not soil a record. D'ye think I stump my bridge for forty-eight hours on end because of the under-writers and the deck hands? Not me, my girl, not me! It's my trade to lay her sweetly in Barcelona bay, and it's my honour to know my work and do it."

He seemed to shrug his shoulder. The girl could not know it was his right hand he flung up to the scarred steel plates above him.

"There's your *Burdock*," he said. "She's your divi-dend grinder; she's my ship. And if I'd thought of no more than your five thousand tons and your forty lives, she'd not be where she is."

He held out his left hand, palm uppermost, and started and blinked when there came no smack of the right fist descending into it.

"There's me talking again," he said. "Never mind, Minnie dear, it's only your old uncle. Let's be back up town."

The wedding day was a Thursday. The ceremony was to take place in the chapel of which David Davis was a member; the subsequent festivities were arranged for at an hotel. It was to be a notable affair, an epoch-maker in the local shipping world, and when all was over there would be time for the newly-wedded to go aboard the *Burdock* and take her out on the tide. Old Captain Price, decorous in stiff black, drove to the church with his son in a two-horse brougham. Neither spoke a word till they were close to the chapel door. Then the old man burst out suddenly:

"For God's sake, Arthur boy, do the right thing by your ship."

Arthur Price was a little moved. "I will, Father," he said. "Here's my hand on it." There was a pause. "Why don't you take my hand, Father?" he asked.

"Eh?" The old man started. "I thought I'd took it, Arthur. I'll be going soft next. Here's the other hand for you."

The reception at the hotel and the breakfast there were notable affairs. Everybody who counted for anything with the hosts was there, and after a little preliminary formality and awkwardness the function grew to animation. The shipping folk of Cardiff know champagne less as a beverage than as a symbol, and there was plenty of it. Serious men became frivolous; David Davis made a speech in Welsh; Minnie glowed and blossomed; Arthur was everybody's friend. The old captain, seated at the bottom of the table with an iron-clad matron on one side and a bored reporter on the other watched him with a groan. The man who was to take the *Burdock* out of dock was drinking. Even one glass at such a time would have breached the old man's code; it was a crime against ship-mastership. But Arthur, with his bride beside him, her brown eyes alight, her shoulder against his shoulder, had gone much further than the one glass. The exhilaration of the day dazzled him; a waiter with a bottle to refill his glass was ever at his shoulder. His voice rattled on untiringly; already the old man saw how the muscles of the jaw were slack and the eyes moved loosely. The young captain had a toast to respond to; he swayed as he stood up to speak, and his tongue stumbled on his consonants. The reporter on Captain Price's left offered him champagne at the moment.

"Take it away," rumbled the old man. "Swill it yourself."

The pressman nodded. "It is pretty shocking stuff," he agreed. "I'm going nap on the coffee myself."

It came to a finish at last. The bride went up to change, and old Captain Price took a cab to the docks. The *Burdock* was smart in new paint, and even the deck hands had been washed for the occasion.

"I'll go down with you a bit," he explained to Sewell, the chief mate. "The pilot'll bring me back. I suppose I can go up to the chart-house?"

"Of course, sir," said Sewell. "If you can't go where you like aboard of us, who can?"

The old man smiled. "That'll be for the captain to say," he answered, and went up the ladder.

She was very smart, the old *Burdock*, and Arthur had made changes in the chart-house, but she had the same feel for her old captain. Under her paint and frills, the steel of her structure was unaltered; the old engines would heave her along; the old seas conspire against her. Shift and bedeck and bedrape her as they might, she was yet the *Burdock*; her lights would run down the Channel with no new consciousness in their stare, and there was work and peril for men aboard of her as of old.

"Ah, Father," said Arthur Price, as he came on the bridge. "Come to shee me chase her roun' the d-dock, eh?" Even as he spoke he tottered. "Damn shlippery deck, eh?" he said. "Well, you'll shee shome shteering, 'tanyrate."

He wiped his forehead and his cap fell off. The old man stooped hurriedly and picked it up for him.

"Brace up, Arthur," he said, in an urgent whisper, "an' let the pilot take her down the dock. For God's sake, don't run any risks."

"I'm captain," said the younger man. "Aren't I Capt'n? Well, then, 'nough said!" He went to the bridge rail.

"All ready, Mish' Mate?" he demanded, and proceeded to get his moorings in.

The mud pilot came to the old captain's side.

"Captain," he said, "that man's drunk."

The old man shuddered a little. "Don't make a noise," he said. "He—he was married to-day."

"Aye." The pilot shook his head. "You know me, Captain; it's not me that would give a son of yours away. But I can't let him bump her about. He isn't you at handling a steamship, and he's drunk."

The old captain turned to him. "Help me out," he said. "Pilot, give me a help in this. I'll stand by him and handy to the telegraph. We'll get her through all right. There's that crowd on the dock"— he signed to the festive guests—"waiting to see him off, and we mustn't make a show of him. And his wife's aboard."

The pilot nodded shortly. "I'm willing."

Arthur, leaning on the rail, was cursing the dock boat at the buoy. The lock was waiting for them, and he lurched to the telegraph, slammed the handle over with a clatter and rang for steam. The pilot and the old man leaned quickly to the indicator; he had ordered full speed ahead.

"Stop her!" snapped the pilot as the decks beneath them pulsed to the awaking engines. Arthur's hand was yet as the handle, but the old man's grip on his wrist was firm, and the bell below clanged again. The young captain wheeled on them furiously.

"Get off my brish," he shouted. "Down with you, th' pair of you." He made to advance on them, those two square old ship-men; he projected a general ruin; but his feet were not his own. He reeled against the rail.

"Port your helm!" commanded the pilot calmly. "Slow ahead!" Old Captain Price rang for him and they began to draw out. Ashore the wedding guests were a flutter of waving handkerchiefs and hats. They thanked God Minnie was not on the bridge. At the rail, Arthur lolled stupidly and seemed to be fighting down a nausea.

"Steady!" came the sure voice of the pilot. "Steady as you go! Stop her!"

Arthur Price slipped then and came to his knees. Ashore, the party was cheering.

"Up with you, Arthur," cried the old man in an agony, "Them people's looking. Stiffen up, my boy."

"Half speed ahead!" droned the pilot, never turning his head.

The old man rattled the handle over and stooped to his son.

"You can lie down when you turn her over to the mate," he said grimly. "Till then you'll stand up and show yourself, if your feet perish under you. I'll hold you."

They were drawing round a tier of big vessels, going cautiously, not with the speed and knife-edge accuracy with which the old man had been wont to take her out, but groping safely through the craft about them. Arthur swayed and smiled and slackened, his head nodding as though in response to the friends on the dock who never abated their farewell clamour. The grip on his arm held him up, for he had weakened on his drink, as excitable men will.

"Starboard!" ordered the pilot, and Captain Price half turned to pass the word. It was then that it happened. The drunken man pivoted where he stood and stumbled sideways, catching himself on the telegraph. The old man snatched him upright, for his knees were melting under him, and from below there came the clang of the bell. Arthur Price had pulled the handle over. Forthwith she quickened; she drove ahead for the stern of the ship she was being conned to clear; her prow was aimed at it, like a descending sword.

"Hard a-port!" roared the pilot, jumping back to

bellow to the wheel. "Spin her round, sheer; over with her!" The wheel engine set up its clatter; with a savage wrench the old captain shook his son to steadiness for an instant and lifted his eyes to see the *Burdock* charging to disaster.

"Stop her!" cried the pilot. "Full astern!"

Captain Price tightened his grip on his son's arm and reached for the handle with his other hand.

Clang! clang! went the deep-toned bell below, and swoosh went the reversed propeller. The pilot's orders rattled like hail on a roof; she came round, and old Captain Price had a glimpse of a knot of frantic men at the taffrail of the ship they barely cleared. Then, slowly they wedged her into the lock-mouth and hauled in.

"Close thing!" said the pilot, panting a little.

The old man let his son lean against the rail, and turned to him.

"P'raps not," he said. "Pilot, what did I ring them engines with?" The other stared. "I had a hold of *him* with this hand of mine; I reached for the handle with my—other—hand."

"But," the pilot was perplexed—"but, Captain, you ain't got no other hand."

"No!" Captain Price shook his head. "But I rang the engines with it, all the same. I rang the *Burdock* out of a bump with it; and——" he hesitated a moment and nodded his head sideways at the limp, lolling body of his son—"I rang his honour off the mud with it."

The pilot cleared his brow; he simply gave the matter up.

"And what about now?" he asked. "He ain't fit to be trusted with her?"

"No," said Captain Price firmly. "He's going to retire from the sea; and till he does, I'll sail as a passenger. And then I'll take the *Burdock* again. *She* don't care about that old spar of mine, the *Burdock* don't."

Three Skeleton Key

My most terrifying experience? Well, one does have
a few in thirty-five years of service in the Lights,
although it's mostly monotonous routine work –
keeping the light in order, making out the reports.

When I was a young man, not very long in the
service, there was an opening in a lighthouse newly
built off the coast of Guiana, on a small rock twenty
miles or so from the mainland. The pay was high, so
in order to reach the sum I had set out to save before
I married, I volunteered for service in the new light.

Three Skeleton Key, the small rock on which the
light stood, bore a bad reputation. It earned its
name from the story of the three convicts who,
escaping from Cayenne in a stolen dugout canoe,
were wrecked on the rock during the night, managed
to escape the sea but eventually died of hunger and
thirst. When they were discovered, nothing remained
but three heaps of bones, picked clean by the birds.
The story was that the three skeletons, gleaming
with phosphorescent light, danced over the small
rock, screaming . . .

But there are many such stories and I did not

give the warnings of the old-timers at the *Isle de Sein* a second thought. I signed up, boarded ship and in a month I was installed at the light.

Picture a grey, tapering cylinder, welded to the solid black rock by iron rods and concrete, rising from a small island twenty-odd miles from land. It lay in the midst of the sea, this island, a small, bare piece of stone, about one hundred and fifty feet long, perhaps forty wide. Small, barely large enough for a man to walk about and stretch his legs at low tide.

This is an advantage one doesn't find in all lights, however, for some of them rise sheer from the waves, with no room for one to move save within the light itself. Still, on our island, one must be careful, for the rocks were treacherously smooth. One misstep and down you would fall into the sea – not that the risk of drowning was so great, but the waters about our island swarmed with huge sharks who kept an eternal patrol around the base of the light.

Still, it was a nice life there. We had enough provisions to last for months, in the event that the sea should become too rough for the supply ship to reach us on schedule. During the day we would work about the light, cleaning the rooms, polishing the metalwork and the lens and reflector of the light itself, and at night we would sit on the gallery and watch our light, a twenty-thousand-candle-power lantern, swinging its strong, white bar of light over the sea from the top of its hundred-and-twenty-foot tower. Some days, when the air would be very clear, we could see the land, a thread-like line to the west. To the east, north and south stretched the ocean. Landsmen, perhaps, would soon have tired of that kind of life, perched on a small island off the coast of South America for eighteen weeks, until one's turn for leave ashore came around. But we liked it there, my two fellowtenders and myself – so much so that, for twenty-two months on end with the exception of shore leaves, I was greatly satisfied with the life on Three Skeleton Key.

I had just returned from my leave at the end of June, that is to say mid-winter in that latitude, and bad settled down to the routine with my two fellow-keepers, a Breton by the name of Le Gleo and the head-keeper Itchoua, a Basque some dozen years or so older than either of us.

Eight days went by as usual, then on the ninth night after my return, Itchoua, who was on night duty, called Le Gleo and me, sleeping in our rooms in the middle of the tower at two in the morning. We rose immediately and climbing the thirty or so steps that led to the gallery, stood beside our chief.

Itchoua pointed, and following his finger, we saw

a big three-master, with all sail set, heading straight for the light. A queer course, for the vessel must have seen us, our light hit her with the glare of day each time it passed over her.

Now, ships were a rare sight in our waters for our light was a warning of treacherous reefs, barely hidden under the surface and running far out to sea. Consequently we were always given a wide berth, especially by sailing vessels, which cannot man-oeuvre as readily as steamers.

No wonder that we were surprised at seeing this three-master heading dead for us in the gloom of early morning. I had immediately recognized her lines, for she stood out plainly, even at the distance of a mile, when our light shone on her.

She was a beautiful ship of some four thousand tons, a fast sailer that had carried cargoes to every part of the world, ploughing the seas unceasingly. By her lines she was identified as Dutch-built, which was understandable as Paramaribo and Dutch Guiana are wry close to Cayenne.

Watching her sailing dead for us, a white wave boiling under her bows, Le Gleo cried out:

'What's wrong with her crew? Are they all drunk or insane? Can't they see us?'

Itchoua nodded soberly, looked at us sharply as

he remarked: 'See us? No doubt – if there is a crew aboard!'

'What do you mean, chief?' Le Gleo had started, turned to the Basque, 'Are you saying that she's the "Flying Dutchman"?'

His sudden fright had been so evident that the older man laughed:

'No, old man, that's not what I meant. If I say that no one's aboard, I mean she's a derelict.'

Then we understood her behaviour. Itchoua was right. For some reason, believing her doomed, her crew had abandoned her. Then she had righted herself and sailed on, wandering with the wind.

The three of us grew tense as the ship seemed about to crash on one of our numerous reefs, but she suddenly lurched with some change of the wind, the yards swung around and the derelict came clumsily about and sailed dead away from us.

In the light of our lantern she seemed so sound, so strong, that Itchoua exclaimed impatiently:

'But why the devil was she abandoned? Nothing is smashed, no sign of fire – and she doesn't sail as if she were taking water.'

Le Gleo waved to the departing ship:

'*Bon voyage!*' he smiled at Itchoua and went on. 'She's leaving us, chief, and now we'll never know what—'

'No she's not!' cried the Basque. 'Look! She's turning!'

As if obeying his words, the derelict three-master stopped, came about and headed for us once more. And for the next four hours the vessel played around us – zig-zagging, coming about, stopping, then suddenly lurching forward. No doubt some freak of current and wind, of which our island was the centre, kept her near us.

Then suddenly, the tropic dawn broke, the sun rose and it was day, and the ship was plainly visible as she sailed past us. Our light extinguished, we returned to the gallery with our glasses and inspected her.

The three of us focused our glasses on her poop, saw standing out sharply, black letters on the white background of a life-ring, the stencilled name:

'*Cornelius-de-Witt, Rotterdam.*'

We had read her lines correctly, she was Dutch. Just then the wind rose and the *Cornelius de Witt* changed course, leaned to port and headed straight for us once more. But this time she was so close that we knew she would not turn in time.

'Thunder!' cried Le Gleo, his Breton soul aching to see a fine ship doomed to smash upon a reef, 'she's going to pile up! She's gone!'

I shook my head:

'Yes, and a shame to see that beautiful ship wreck herself. And we're helpless.'

There was nothing we could do but watch. A ship sailing with all sail spread, creaming the sea with her forefoot as she runs before the wind, is one of the most beautiful sights in the world – but this time I could feel the tears stinging my eyes as I saw this fine ship headed for her doom.

All this time our glasses were riveted on her and we suddenly cried out together:

'The rats!'

Now we knew why this ship, in perfect condition, was sailing without her crew aboard. They had been driven out by the rats. Not those poor specimens of rats you see ashore, barely reaching the length of one foot from their trembling noses to the tip of their skinny tails, wretched creatures that dodge and hide at the mere sound of a footfall.

No, these were ships' rats, huge, wise creatures, born on the sea, sailing all over the world on ships, transferring to other, larger ships as they multiply. There is as much difference between the rats of the land and these maritime rats as between a fishing smack and an armoured cruiser.

The rats of the sea are fierce, bold animals. Large, strong and intelligent, clannish and seawise, able to put the best of mariners to shame with their

knowledge of the sea, their uncanny ability to fore-
tell the weather.

And they are brave, the rats, and vengeful. If you
so much as harm one, his sharp cry will bring hordes
of his fellows to swarm over you, tear you and not
cease until your flesh has been stripped from the
bones.

The ones on this ship, the rats of Holland, are the
worst, superior to other rats of the sea as their breth-
ren are to the land rats. There is a well-known tale
about these animals.

A Dutch captain, thinking to protect his cargo,
brought aboard his ship – not cats – but two terriers,
dogs trained in the hunting, fighting and killing of
vicious rats. By the time the ship, sailing from Rotterdam, had passed the Ostend light, the dogs were
gone and never seen again. In twenty-four hours they
had been overwhelmed, killed, and eaten by the rats.

At times, when the cargo docs not suffice, the rats
attack the crew, either driving them from the ship
or eating them alive. And studying the *Cornelius de
Witt*, I turned sick, for her small boats were all in
place. She had not been abandoned.

Over her bridge, on her deck, in the rigging, on
every visible spot, the ship was a writhing mass – a
starving army coming towards us aboard a vessel
gone mad!

Our island was a small spot in that immense stretch of sea. The ship could have grazed us, passed to port or starboard with its ravening cargo – but no, she came for us at full speed, as if she were leading the regatta at a race, and impaled herself on a sharp point of rock.

There was a dull shock as her bottom stove in, then a horrible crackling as the three masts went overboard at once, as if cut down with one blow of some gigantic sickle. A sighing groan came as the water rushed into the ship, then she split in two and sank like a stone.

But the rats did not drown. Not these fellows! As much at home in the sea as any fish, they formed ranks in the water, heads lifted, tails stretched out, paws paddling. And half of them, those from the forepart of the ship, sprang along the masts and onto the rocks in the instant before she sank. Before we had time even to move, nothing remained of the three-master save some pieces of wreckage floating on the surface and an army of rats covering the rocks left bare by the receding tide.

Thousands of heads rose, felt the wind and we were scented, seen! To them we were fresh meat, after possible weeks of starving. There came a scream, composed of innumerable screams, sharper than the howl of a saw attacking a bar of iron, and in the one motion, every rat leaped to attack the tower!

We barely had time to leap back, close the door leading onto the gallery, descend the stairs and shut every window tightly. Luckily the door at the base of the light, which we never could have reached in time, was of bronze set in granite and was tightly closed.

The horrible band, in no measurable time, had swarmed up and over the tower as if it had been a tree, piled on the embrasures of the windows, scraped at the glass with thousands of claws, covered the lighthouse with a furry mantle and reached the top of the tower, filling the gallery and piling atop the lantern.

Their teeth grated as they pressed against the glass of the lantern-room, where they could plainly see us, though they could not reach us. A few millimetres of glass, luckily very strong, separated our faces from their gleaming, beady eyes, their sharp claws and teeth. Their odour filled the tower, poisoned our lungs and rasped our nostrils with a pestilential, nauseating smell. And there we were, scaled alive in our own light, prisoners of a horde of starving rats.

That first night, the tension was so great that we could not sleep. Every moment, we felt that some opening had been made, some window given away, and that our horrible besiegers were pouring through the breach. The rising tide, chasing those of the rats which had stayed on the bare rocks, increased the numbers clinging to the walls, piled on the balcony – so much so that clusters of rats clinging to one another hung from the lantern and the gallery.

With the coming of darkness we lit the light and the turning beam completely maddened the beasts. As the light turned, it successively blinded thousands of rats crowded against the glass, while the dark side of the lantern-room gleamed with thousands of points of light, burning like the eyes of jungle beasts in the night.

All the while we could hear the enraged scraping of claws against the stone and glass, while the chorus of cries was so loud that we had to shout to hear one another. From time to time, some of the rats fought among themselves and a dark cluster would detach itself, falling into the sea like a ripe fruit from a tree. Then we would see phosphorescent streaks as triangular fins slashed the water – sharks, permanent guardians of our rock, feasting on our jailors.

The next day we were calmer, and amused ourselves teasing the rats, placing our faces against the glass which separated us. They could not fathom the invisible barrier which separated them from us and we laughed as we watched them leaping against the heavy glass.

But the day after that, we realized how serious our position was. The air was foul, even the heavy smell of oil within our stronghold could not dominate the fetid odour of the beasts massed around us. And there was no way of admitting fresh air without also admitting the rats.

The morning of the fourth day, at early dawn, I saw the wooden framework of my window, eaten away from the outside, sagging inwards. I called my comrades and the three of us fastened a sheet of tin in the opening, sealing it tightly. When we had completed the task. Itchoua turned to us and said dully:

'Well – the supply boat came thirteen days ago, and she won't be back for twenty-nine.' He pointed at the white metal plate sealing the opening through the granite – 'If that gives way' – he shrugged – 'they can change the name of this place to Six Skeletons Key.'

The next six days and seven nights, our only distraction was watching the rats whose holds were insecure, fall a hundred and twenty feet into the maws of the sharks – but they were so many that we could not see any diminution in their numbers.

Thinking to calm ourselves and pass the time, we attempted to count them, but we soon gave up. They moved incessantly, never still. Then we tried identifying them, naming them.

One of them, larger than the others, who seemed to lead them in their rushes against the glass separating us, we named 'Nero'; and there were several others whom we had learned to distinguish through various peculiarities.

But the thought of our bones joining those of the convicts was always in the back of our minds. And the gloom of our prison fed these thoughts, for the interior of the light was almost completely dark, as we had to seal every window in the same fashion as mine, and the only space that still admitted daylight was the glassed-in lantern-room at the very top of the tower.

Then Le Gleo became morose and had nightmares in which he would see the three skeletons dancing around him, gleaming coldly, seeking to grasp him. His maniacal, raving descriptions were so vivid that Itchoua and I began seeing them also.

It was a living nightmare, the raging cries of the rats as they swarmed over the light, mad with hunger; the sickening, strangling odour of their bodies –

True, there is a way of signalling from lighthouses. But to reach the mast on which to hang the signal we would have to go out on the gallery where the rats were.

There was only one thing left to do. After debating all of the ninth day, we decided not to light the lantern that night. This is the greatest breach of our service, never committed as long as the tenders of the light are alive; for the light is something sacred, warning ships of danger in the night. Either the light gleams, a quarter-hour after sundown, or no one is left alive to light it.

Well, that night, Three Skeleton Light was dark, and all the men were alive. At the risk of causing ship to crash on our reefs, we left it unlit, for we were worn out – going mad!

At two in the morning, while Itchoua was dozing in his room, the sheet of metal sealing his window gave way. The chief had just time enough to leap to his feet and cry for help, the rats swarming over him.

But Le Gleo and I, who had been watching from the lantern-room, got to him immediately, and the three of us battled with the horde of maddened rats which flowed through the gaping window. They bit, we struck them down with our knives – and retreated.

We locked the door of the room on them, but before we had time to bind our wounds, the door was eaten through, and gave way and we retreated up the stairs, fighting off the rats that leaped on us from the knee-deep swarm.

I do not remember, to this day, how we ever

managed to escape. All I can remember is wading through them up the stairs, striking them off as they swarmed over us; and then we found ourselves, bleeding from innumerable bites, our clothes shredded, sprawled across the trapdoor in the floor of the lantern-room – without food or drink. Luckily, the trapdoor was metal set into the granite with iron bolts.

The rats occupied the entire light beneath us, and on the floor of our retreat by some twenty of their fellows, who had gotten in with us before the trapdoor closed, and whom we had killed with our knives. Below us, in the tower, we could hear the screams of the rats as they devoured everything edible that they found. Those on the outside squealed in reply, and writhed in a horrible curtain as they stared at us through the glass of the lantern-room.

Itchoua sat up, stared silently at his blood trickling from the wounds on his limbs and body, and running in thin streams on the floor around him. Le Gleo, who was in as bad a state (and so was I, for that matter) stared at the chief and me vacantly, started as his gaze swung to the multitude of rats against the glass, then suddenly began laughing horribly:

'Hee! Hee! The Three Skeletons! Hee! Hee!

The Three Skeletons are now *six* skeletons! *Six* skeletons!'

He threw his head back and howled, his eyes glared, a trickle of saliva running from the corners of his mouth and thinning the blood flowing over his chest. I shouted to him to shut up, but he did not hear me, so I did the only thing I could to quiet him – I swung the back of my hand across his face.

The howling stopped suddenly, his eyes swung around the room, then he bowed his head and began weeping softly, like a child.

Our darkened light had been noticed from the mainland, and as dawn was breaking the patrol was there, to investigate the failure of our light. Looking through my binoculars, I could see the horrified expression on the faces of the officers and crew when, the daylight strengthening, they saw the light completely covered by a seething mass of rats. They thought, as I afterwards found out, that we had been eaten alive.

But the rats had also seen the ship, or had scented the crew. As the ship drew nearer, a solid phalanx left the light, plunged into the water and, swimming out, attempted to board her. They would have succeeded, as the ship was hove to, but the engineer connected his steam to hose on the deck and scalded the head of the attacking column, which slowed them up long enough for the ship to get under way and leave the rats behind.

Then the sharks took part. Belly up, mouths gaping, they arrived in swarms and scooped up the rats, sweeping through them like a sickle through wheat. That was one day that sharks really served a useful purpose.

The remaining rats turned tail, swam to the shore and emerged dripping. As they neared the light, their comrades greeted them with shrill cries, with what sounded like a derisive note predominating. They answered angrily and mingled with their fellows. From the several tussles that broke out, they resented being ridiculed for their failure to capture the ship.

But all this did nothing to get us out of our jail. The small ship could not approach, but steamed around the light at a safe distance, and the tower must have seemed fantastic, some weird, many-mouthed beast hurling defiance at them.

Finally, seeing the rats running in and out of the tower through the door and the windows, those on the ship decided that we had perished and were about to leave when Itchoua, regaining his senses, thought of using the light as a signal. He lit it and, using a plank placed and withdrawn before the beam to form the dots and dashes, quickly sent our story to those on the vessel.

Our reply came quickly. When they understood our position, how we could not get rid of the rats, Le Gleo's mind going fast, Itchoua and myself covered with bites; cornered in the lantern-room without food or water, they had a signalman send us their reply.

His arms, swinging like those of a windmill, he quickly spelled out:

'Don't give up, hang on a little longer! We'll get you out of this!'

Then she turned and steamed at top speed for the coast, leaving us little reassured.

She was back at noon, accompanied by the supply ship, two small coastguard boats, and the fire boat – a small squadron. At twelve-thirty the battle was on.

After a short reconnaissance, the fire boat picked her way slowly through the reefs until she was close to us, then turned her powerful jet of water on the rats. The heavy stream tore the rats from their places, hurled them screaming into the water where the sharks gulped them down. But for every ten that were dislodged, seven swam ashore, and the stream could do nothing to the rats within the tower. Furthermore, some of them, instead of returning to the rocks, boarded the fire boat and the men were forced to battle them hand to hand. They were true rats of Holland, fearing no man, fighting for the right to live!

Nightfall came, and it was as if nothing had been done, the rats were still in possession. One of the patrol boats stayed by the island, the rest of the flotilla departed for the coast. We had to spend another night in our prison. Le Gleo was sitting on the floor, babbling about skeletons and as I turned to Itchoua, he fell unconscious from his wounds. I was in no better shape and could feel my blood flaming with fever.

Somehow the night dragged by, and the next afternoon I saw a tug, accompanied by the fire boat, come from the mainland with a huge barge in tow. Through my glasses, I saw that the barge was filled with meat.

Risking the treacherous reefs, the tug dragged the barge as close to the island as possible. To the last rat, our besiegers deserted the rock, swam out and boarded the barge reeking with the scent of freshly cut meat. The tug dragged the barge about a mile from shore, where the fire boat drenched the barge with gasoline. A well-placed incendiary shell from the patrol boat set her on fire. The barge was covered with flames immediately and the rats took to the water in swarms, but the patrol boat bombarded them with shrapnel from a safe distance, and the sharks finished off the survivors.

A whaleboat from the patrol boat took us off the island and left three men to replace us. By nightfall we were in the hospital in Cayenne. What became of my friends?

Well, Le Gleo's mind had cracked and he was raving mad. They sent him back to France and locked turn up in an asylum, the poor devil; Itchoua died within a week; a rat's bite is dangerous in that hot, humid climate, and infection sets in rapidly.

As for me – when they fumigated the light and repaired the damage done by the rats, I resumed my service there. Why not? No reason why such an incident should keep me from finishing out my service there, is there?

Besides – I told you I liked the place – to be truthful, I've never had a post as pleasant as that one, and when my time came to leave it forever, I tell you that I almost wept as Three Skeleton Key disappeared below the horizon.

C. S. FORESTER

Hornblower and the Widow McCool

The Channel fleet was taking shelter at last. The
roaring westerly gales had worked up to such a pitch
that timber and canvas and cordage could withstand
them no longer, and nineteen ships of the line and
seven frigates, with Admiral Lord Bridport flying his
flag in H.M.S. *Royal George*, had momentarily abandoned that watch over Brest which they had
maintained for six years. Now they were rounding
Berry Head and dropping anchor in the shelter of
Tor Bay.

A landsman, with that wind shrieking round him,
might be pardoned for wondering how much shelter
was to be found there, but to the weary and weather-
beaten crews who had spent so long tossing in the
Biscay waves and clawing away from the rocky coast
of Brittany, that foam-whitened anchorage was like
paradise. Boats could even be sent in to Brixham
and Torquay to return with letters and fresh water;
in most of the ships, officers and men had gone for
three months without either. Even on that winter
day there was intense physical pleasure in opening
the throat and pouring down it a draught of fresh

clear water, so different from the stinking green liquid doled out under guard yesterday.

The junior lieutenant in H.M.S. *Renown* was walking the deck muffled in his heavy pea-jacket while his ship wallowed at her anchor. The piercing wind set his eyes watering, but he continually gazed through his telescope nevertheless; for, as signal lieutenant, he was responsible for the rapid reading and transmission of messages, and this was a likely moment for orders to be given regarding sick and stores, and for captains and admirals to start chattering together, for invitations to dinner to be passed back and forth, and even for news to be disseminated.

He watched a small boat claw its way towards the ship from the French prize the fleet had snapped up yesterday on its way up-channel. Hart, master's mate, had been sent on board from the *Renown*, as prizemaster, miraculously making the perilous journey. Now here was Hart, with the prize safely anchored amid the fleet, returning on board to make some sort of report. That hardly seemed likely to be of interest to a signal lieutenant, but Hart appeared excited as he came on board, and hurried below with his news after reporting himself in the briefest terms to the officer of the watch. But only a very few minutes passed before the signal lieutenant found himself called upon to be most active.

It was Captain Sawyer himself who came on deck, Hart following him, to supervise the transmission of the messages. "Mr. Hornblower!"

"Sir!"

"Kindly send this signal."

It was for the admiral himself, from the captain; that part was easy; only two hoists were necessary to say "*Renown* to Flag". And there were other technical terms which could be quickly expressed—"prize" and "French" and "brig"—but there were names which would have to be spelled out letter for letter. "Prize is French national brig *Espérance II* having on board Barry McCool."

"Mr. James!" bellowed Hornblower. The signal midshipman was waiting at his elbow, but midshipmen should always be bellowed at, especially by a lieutenant with a very new commission.

Hornblower reeled off the numbers, and the signal went soaring up to the yardarm; the signal halyards vibrated wildly as the gale tore at the flags. Captain Sawyer waited on deck for the reply; this business must be important. Hornblower read the message again, for until that moment he had only studied it as something to be transmitted. But even on re-reading it he did not know why the message should be important. Until three months before, he had been a prisoner in Spanish hands for two weary years, and there were gaps in his knowledge of recent history. The name of Barry McCool meant nothing to him.

On the other hand, it seemed to mean a great deal to the admiral, for hardly had sufficient time elapsed for the message to be carried below to him than a question soared up to the *Royal George's* yardarm.

"Flag to *Renown*," Hornblower read those flags as they broke and was instantly ready for the rest of the message. "Is McCool alive?"

"Reply affirmative," said Captain Sawyer.

And the affirmative had hardly been hoisted before the next signal was fluttering in the *Royal George*.

"Have him on board at once. Court martial will assemble."

A court martial! Who on earth was this man McCool? A deserter? The capture of a mere deserter would not be a matter for the commander in chief. A traitor? Strange that a traitor should be court-martialled in the fleet. But there it was.

A word from the captain sent Hart scurrying overside to bring this mysterious prisoner on board, while signal after signal went up from the *Royal George* convening the court martial in the *Renown*.

Hornblower was kept busy enough reading the messages; he had only a glance to spare when Hart had his prisoner and his sea chest hoisted up over the port side. A youngish man, tall and slender, his hands were tied behind him—which was why he had to be hoisted in—and he was hatless, so that his long red hair streamed in the wind. He wore a blue uniform with red facings—a French infantry uniform, apparently. The name, the uniform and the red hair combined to give Hornblower his first insight into the situation. McCool must be an Irishman.

While Hornblower had been a prisoner in Ferrol, there had been, he knew, a bloody rebellion in Ireland. Irishmen who had escaped had taken service with France in large numbers. This must be one of them, but it hardly explained why the admiral should take it upon himself to try him instead of handing him over to the civil authorities.

Hornblower had to wait an hour for the explanation, until, at two bells in the next watch, dinner was served in the gun room.

"There'll be a pretty little ceremony tomorrow morning," said Clive, the surgeon. He put his hand to his neck in a gesture which Hornblower thought hideous.

"I hope the effect will be salutary," said Roberts, the second lieutenant. The foot of the table, where he sat, was for the moment the head, because Buckland, the first lieutenant, was absent attending to the preparations for the court martial.

"But why should we hang him?" asked Hornblower.

Roberts rolled an eye on him.

"Deserter," he said, and then went on. "Of course, you're a newcomer. I entered him myself, into this very ship, in '98. Hart spotted him at once."

"But I thought he was a rebel?"

"A rebel as well," said Roberts. "The quickest way out of Ireland—the only way, in fact—in '98 was to join the armed forces."

"I see," said Hornblower.

"We got a hundred hands that autumn," said Smith, another lieutenant.

And no questions would be asked, thought Hornblower. His country, fighting for her life, needed seamen as a drowning man needs air, and was prepared to make them out of any raw material that presented itself.

"McCool deserted one dark night when we were becalmed off the Pointe de Penmarch in Brittany," explained Roberts. "Got through a lower gunport with a grating to float him. We thought he was drowned until news came through from Paris that he was there, up to his old games. He boasted of what he'd done—that's how we knew him to be O'Shaughnessy, as he called himself when we had him."

"Wolfe Tone had a French uniform," said Smith. "And they'd have strung him up if he hadn't cut his own throat first."

"Uniform only aggravates the offence when he's a deserter," said Roberts.

Hornblower had much to think about. First there was the nauseating thought that there would be an execution in the morning. Then there was this eternal Irish problem, about which the more he thought the more muddled he became. If just the bare facts were considered, there could be no problem. In the world at the moment, Ireland could choose only between the domination of England and the domination of France; no other possibility existed in a world at war. And it seemed unbelievable that anyone would wish to escape from English overlordship—absentee landlords and Catholic disabilities notwithstanding—in order to submit to the rapacity and cruelty and venality of the French republic. To risk one's life to effect such an exchange would be a most illogical thing to do, but logic, Hornblower concluded sadly, had no bearing upon patriotism, and the bare facts were the least considerable factors.

And in the same way the English methods were subject to criticism as well. There could be no doubt that the Irish people looked upon Wolfe Tone and Fitzgerald as martyrs, and would look upon McCool in the same light. There was nothing so effective as a few martyrdoms to ennoble and invigorate a cause.

The hanging of McCool would merely be adding fuel to the fire that England sought to extinguish. Two peoples actuated by the most urgent of motives—self-preservation and patriotism—were at grips in a struggle which could have no satisfactory ending for a long time to come.

Buckland, the first lieutenant, came into the gun room with the preoccupied look commonly worn by first lieutenants with a weight of responsibility on their shoulders. He ran his glance over the assembled company, and all the junior officers, sensing that unpleasant duties were about to be allocated, did their unobtrusive best not to meet his eye. Inevitably it was the name of the most junior lieutenant which rose to Buckland's lips.

"Mr. Hornblower," he said.

"Sir!" replied Hornblower, doing his best now to keep resignation out of his voice.

"I am going to make you responsible for the prisoner."

"Sir?" said Hornblower, with a different intonation.

"Hart will be giving evidence at the court martial," explained Buckland—it was a vast condescension that he should deign to explain at all. "The master-at-arms is a fool, as you know. I want McCool brought up for trial safe and sound, and I want him kept safe and sound afterwards. I'm repeating the captain's own words, Mr. Hornblower."

"Aye, aye, sir," said Hornblower, for there was nothing else to be said.

"No Wolfe Tone tricks with McCool," said Smith.

Wolfe Tone had cut his own throat the night before he was due to be hanged, and had died in agony a week later.

"Ask me for anything you may need, Mr. Hornblower," said Buckland.

"Aye, aye, sir."

"Side boys!" suddenly roared a voice on deck overhead, and Buckland hurried out; the approach of an officer of rank meant that the court martial was beginning to assemble.

Hornblower's chin was on his breast. It was a

hard, unrelenting world, and he was an officer in the hardest and most unrelenting service in that world—a service in which a man could no more say "I cannot" than he could say "I dare not".

"Bad luck, Horny," said Smith, with surprising gentleness, and there were other murmurs of sympathy from round the table.

"Obey orders, young man," said Roberts quietly.

Hornblower rose from his chair. He could not trust himself to speak, so that it was with a hurried bow that he quitted the company at the table.

"'E's 'ere, safe an' sound, Mr. 'Ornblower," said the master-at-arms, halting in the darkness of the lower 'tween decks.

A marine sentry at the door moved out of the way, and the master-at-arms shone the light of his candle lantern on a keyhole in a door and inserted the key.

"I put 'im in this empty storeroom, sir," went on the master-at-arms. "'E's got two of my corporals along with 'im."

The door opened, revealing the light of another candle lantern. The air inside the room was foul; McCool was sitting on a chest, while two of the ship's corporals sat on the deck with their backs to the bulkhead. The corporals rose at an officer's entrance, but even so, there was almost no room for the two newcomers.

Hornblower cast a vigilant eye round the arrangements. There appeared to be no chance of escape or suicide. In the end, he steeled himself to meet McCool's eyes.

"I have been put in charge of you," he said.

"That is most gratifying to me, Mr.—Mr.——" said McCool, rising from the chest.

"Hornblower."

"I am delighted to make your acquaintance, Mr. Hornblower."

McCool spoke in a cultured voice, with only enough of Ireland in it to betray his origin. He had tied back the red locks into a neat queue, and even in the faint candlelight his blue eyes gave strange reflections.

"Is there anything you need?" asked Hornblower.

"I could eat and I could drink," replied McCool. "Seeing that nothing whatsoever has passed my lips since *Espérance II* was captured."

That was yesterday. The man had had neither food nor water for more than twenty-four hours.

"I will see to it," said Hornblower. "Anything more?"

"A mattress or a cushion—something on which I can sit," said McCool. He waved a hand towards his sea chest. "I bear an honoured name, but I have no desire to bear it imprinted on my person."

The sea chest was of a rich mahogany. The lid was a thick slab of wood whose surface had been chiselled down to leave his name, B. I. McCool, standing out in high relief.

"I'll send you in a mattress, too," said Hornblower.

A lieutenant in uniform appeared at the door.

"I'm Payne, on the admiral's staff," he explained to Hornblower. "I have orders to search this man."

"Certainly," said Hornblower.

"You have my permission," said McCool.

The master-at-arms and his assistants had to quit the crowded little room to enable Payne to do his work, while Hornblower stood in the corner and watched.

Payne was quick and efficient. He made McCool strip to the skin and examined his clothes with care—seams, linings and buttons. He crumpled each portion carefully, with his ear to the material, apparently to hear if there were papers concealed inside. Then he knelt down to the chest; the key was already in the lock, and he swung it open. Uniforms, shirts, underclothing, gloves; each article was taken out, examined and laid aside. There were two small portraits of children, to which Payne gave special attention without discovering anything.

"The things you are looking for," said McCool, "were all dropped overside before the prize crew could reach *Espérance II*. You'll find nothing to betray my fellow countrymen, and you may as well save yourself that trouble."

"You can put your clothes on again," said Payne curtly to McCool. He nodded to Hornblower and hurried out again.

"A man whose politeness is quite overwhelming," said McCool, buttoning his breeches.

"I'll attend to your requests," said Hornblower.

He paused only long enough to enjoin the strictest vigilance on the master-at-arms and the ship's corporals before hastening away to give orders for McCool to be given food and water, and he returned quickly.

McCool drank his quart of water eagerly, and made an effort to eat the ship's biscuit and meat.

"No knife. No fork," he commented.

"No," replied Hornblower in a tone devoid of expression.

"I understand."

It was strange to stand there gazing down at this man who was going to die tomorrow, biting not very efficiently at the lump of tough meat which he held to his teeth.

The bulkhead against which Hornblower leaned

vibrated slightly, and the sound of a gun came faintly down to them. It was the signal that the court martial was about to open.

"Do we go?" asked McCool.

"Yes."

"Then I can leave this delicious food without any breach of good manners."

They climbed the ladders to the main deck, two marines leading, McCool following them, Hornblower following him, and two ship's corporals bringing up the rear.

"I have frequently traversed these decks," said McCool, looking round him, "with less ceremonial."

Hornblower was watching carefully lest he should break away and throw himself into the sea.

The court martial had begun. There was much gold lace and curt efficient routine, as the *Renown* swung to her anchors and the timbers of the ship transmitted the sound of the rigging vibrating in the gale. Evidence of identification came first, followed by a series of curt questions.

"Nothing I could say would be listened to amid the emblems of tyranny," said McCool in reply to the president of the court.

It needed no more than fifteen minutes to

condemn a man to death: "The sentence of this court is that you, Barry Ignatius McCool, be hanged by the neck——"

The storeroom to which Hornblower escorted McCool back was now a condemned cell. A hurrying midshipman asked for Hornblower almost as soon as they arrived there.

"Captain's compliments, sir, and he'd like to speak to you."

"Very good," said Hornblower.

"The Admiral's with him, sir," added the midshipman in a burst of confidence.

Admiral the Honourable Sir William Cornwallis was indeed in the captain's cabin, along with Payne and Captain Sawyer. He went straight to the point the moment Hornblower had been presented to him.

"You're the officer charged with carrying out the execution?" he asked.

"Yes, sir."

"Now look'ee here, young sir——"

Cornwallis was a popular admiral, strict but kindly, and of unflinching courage and towering professional ability. Under his nickname of "Billy Blue" he was the hero of uncounted anecdotes and ballads. But having got so far in what he was intending to say, he betrayed a hesitation alien to his character. Hornblower waited for him to continue.

"Look'ee here," said Cornwallis again. "There's to be no speechifying when he's strung up."

"No, sir?" said Hornblower.

"A quarter of the hands in this ship are Irish," went on Cornwallis. "I'd as lief have a light taken into the magazine as have McCool make a speech to 'em."

"I understand, sir," said Hornblower.

But there was a ghastly routine about executions. From time immemorial the condemned man had been allowed to address his last words to the onlookers.

"String him up," said Cornwallis, "and that'll show 'em what to expect if they run off. But once let him open his mouth—— That fellow has the gift of the gab, and we'll have this crew unsettled for the next six months."

"Yes, sir."

"So see to it, young sir. Fill him full o' rum, perhaps. But let him speak at your peril."

"Aye, aye, sir."

Payne followed Hornblower out of the cabin when he was dismissed.

"You might stuff his mouth with oakum," he suggested. "With his hands tied he could not get it out."

"I've found a priest for him," went on Payne, "but he's Irish too. We can't rely on him to tell McCool to keep his mouth shut."

"Yes," said Hornblower.

"McCool's devilish cunning. No doubt he'd throw everything overboard before they captured him."

"What was he intending to do?" asked Hornblower.

"Land in Ireland and stir up fresh trouble. Lucky we caught him. Lucky, for that matter, we could charge him with desertion and make a quick business of it."

"Yes," said Hornblower.

"Don't rely on making him drunk," said Payne, "although that was Billy Blue's advice. Drunk or sober, these Irishmen can always talk. I've given you the best hint."

"Yes," said Hornblower, concealing a shudder.

He went back into the condemned cell like a man condemned himself. McCool was sitting on the straw mattress Hornblower had had sent in, the two ship's corporals still had him under their observation.

"Here comes Jack Ketch," said McCool with a smile that almost escaped appearing forced.

Hornblower plunged into the matter in hand; he could see no tactful way of approach.

"Tomorrow——" he said.

"Yes, tomorrow?"

"Tomorrow you are to make no speeches," he said.

"None? No farewell to my countrymen?"

"No."

"You are robbing a condemned man of his last privilege."

"I have my orders," said Hornblower.

"And you propose to enforce them?"

"Yes."

"May I ask how?"

"I can stop your mouth with tow," said Hornblower brutally.

McCool looked at the pale, strained face. "You do not appear to me to be the ideal executioner," said McCool, and then a new idea seemed to strike him. "Supposing I were to save you that trouble?"

"How?"

"I could give you my parole to say nothing."

Hornblower tried to conceal his doubts as to whether he could trust a fanatic about to die.

"Oh, you wouldn't have to trust my bare word," said McCool bitterly. "We can strike a bargain, if you will. You need not carry out your half unless I have already carried out mine."

"A bargain?"

"Yes. Allow me to write to my widow. Promise me to send her the letter and my sea chest here—you can see it is of sentimental value—and I, on my side, promise to say no word from the time of leaving this place here until—until——" Even McCool faltered at that point. "Is that explicit enough?"

"Well——" said Hornblower.

"You can read the letter," added McCool. "You saw that other gentleman search my chest. Even though you send these things to Dublin, you can be sure that they contain nothing of what you would call treason."

"I'll read the letter before I agree," said Hornblower.

It seemed a way out of a horrible situation. There would be small trouble about finding a coaster destined for Dublin; for a few shillings he could send letter and chest there.

"I'll send you in pen and ink and paper," said Hornblower.

It was time to make the other hideous preparations: to have a whip rove at the portside fore yardarm, and to see that the line ran easily through the block; to weight the line and mark a ring with chalk on the gangway where the end rested; to see that the noose ran smooth; to arrange with Buckland for ten men to be detailed to pull when the time came. Hornblower went through it all like a man in a nightmare.

Back in the condemned cell, McCool was pale and wakeful, but he could still force a smile.

"You can see that I had trouble wooing the muse," he said.

At his feet lay a couple of sheets of paper, and Hornblower, glancing at them, could see that they were covered with what looked like attempts at writing poetry. The erasures and alterations were numerous.

"But here is my fair copy," said McCool, handing over another sheet.

My darling wife, the letter began. *It is hard to find words to say farewell to my dearest . . .*

It was not easy for Hornblower to force himself to read that letter. It was as if he had to peer through a mist to make out the words. But they were only the words of a man writing to his beloved, whom he would never again see. That at least was plain. He compelled himself to read through the affectionate sentences. At the end it said:

> *I append a poor poem by which in the years to come you may remember me, my dearest love. And now goodbye, until we shall be together in Heaven.*
>
> > *Your husband, faithful unto death,*
> >
> > *Barry Ignatius McCool.*

Then came the poem—

> *Ye heavenly powers! Stand by me when I die!*
> *The bee ascends before my rolling eye.*
> *Life still goes on within the heartless town.*
> *Dark forces claim my soul. So strike 'em down.*
> *The sea will rise, the sea will fall. So turn*
> *Full circle. Turn again. And then will burn*
> *The lambent flames while hell will lift its head.*
> *So pray for me while I am numbered with the dead.*

Hornblower read through the turgid lines and puzzled over their obscure imagery. But he wondered if he would be able to write a single line that would make sense if he knew he was going to die in a few hours.

"The superscription is on the other side," said McCool, and Hornblower turned the sheet over.

The letter was addressed to the Widow McCool, in some street in Dublin.

"Will you accept my word now?" asked McCool.

"Yes," said Hornblower.

The horrible thing was done in the grey hours of the morning.

"Hands to witness punishment."

The pipes twittered and the hands assembled in the waist, facing forward. The marines stood in lines across the deck. There were masses and masses of white faces, which Hornblower saw when he brought McCool up from below. There was a murmur when McCool appeared.

Around the ship lay boats from all the rest of the fleet, filled with men—men sent to witness the punishment, but ready also to storm the ship should the crew stir. McCool stood in the chalk ring on the gangway. Then came the signal gun, and the rush of feet as the ten hands heaved away on the line. And McCool died, as he had promised, without saying a word.

The body hung at the yardarm, and as the ship rolled in the swell that came round Berry Head, so the body swung and dangled, doomed to hang there until nightfall, while Hornblower, sick and pale, began to seek out a coaster which planned to call at

Dublin from Brixham, so that he could fulfil his half of the bargain. But he could not fulfil it immediately; nor did the dead body hang there for its allotted time.

The wind was backing northerly and was showing signs of moderating. A westerly gale would keep the French fleet shut up in Brest; a northerly one might well bring them out, and the Channel fleet must hurry to its post again. Signals flew from the flagships.

"Hands to the capstan!" bellowed the bosuns' mates in twenty-four ships. "Hands make sail!"

With double-reefed topsails set, the ships of the Channel fleet formed up and began their long slant down-Channel. In the *Renown* it had been "Mr. Hornblower, see that *that* is disposed of". While the hands laboured at the capstan the corpse was lowered from the yardarm and sewn into a weighted bit of sailcloth. Clear of Berry Head it was cast overside without ceremony or prayer. McCool had died a felon's death and must be given a felon's burial. And, close-hauled, the big ships clawed their way back to their posts amid the rocks and currents of the Brittany coast. And on board the *Renown* there was one unhappy lieutenant, at least, plagued by dreadful memories.

In the tiny cabin which he shared with Smith

there was something that kept Hornblower continually reminded of that morning: the mahogany chest with the name "B. I. McCOOL" in high relief on the lid. And in Hornblower's letter-case lay that last, letter and the rambling, delirious poem. Hornblower could send neither on to the widow until the *Renown* should return again to an English harbour, and he was irked that he had not yet fulfilled his half of the bargain. The sight of the chest under his cot jarred on his nerves; its presence in their little cabin irritated Smith.

Hornblower could not rid his memory of McCool; nor, beating about in a ship of the line on the dreary work of blockade, was there anything to distract him from his obsession. Spring was approaching and the weather was moderating.

When he opened his leather case and found that letter staring at him again, he felt undiminished that revulsion of spirit. He turned the sheet over; in the half dark of that little cabin he could hardly read the gentle words of farewell. He knew that strange poem almost by heart, and he peered at it again, sacrilege though it seemed to try to analyse the thoughts of the brave and frightened man who had written it during his final agony of spirit. *"The bee ascends before my rolling eye."* What could possibly be the feeling that inspired that strange imagery? *"Turn full circle. Turn again."* Why should the heavenly powers do that?

A startling thought began to wake to life in Hornblower's mind. The letter, with its tender phrasing, had been written without correction or erasure. But this poem; Hornblower remembered the discarded sheets covered with scribbling. It had been written with care and attention. A madman, a man distraught with trouble, might produce a meaningless poem with such prolonged effort, but then he would not have written that letter. Perhaps—perhaps——

Hornblower sat up straight instead of lounging back on his cot. *"So strike 'em down."* There was no apparent reason why McCool should have written *"'em"* instead of *"them"*. Hornblower mouthed the words. To say "them" did not mar either euphony or rhythm. There might be a code. But then why the chest? Why had McCool asked for the chest to be forwarded with its uninteresting contents of clothing? There were two portraits of children; they could easily have been made into a package. The chest with its solid slabs of mahogany and its raised name was a handsome piece of furniture, but it was all very puzzling.

With the letter still in his hand, he got down from the cot and dragged out the chest. B. I. McCOOL.

Barry Ingatius McCool. Payne had gone carefully through the contents of the chest. Hornblower unlocked it and glanced inside again; he could see nothing meriting particular attention, and he closed the lid again and turned the key. B. I. McCOOL. A secret compartment! In a fever, Hornblower opened the chest again, flung out the contents and examined sides and bottom. It called for only the briefest examination to assure him that there was no room there for anything other than a microscopic secret compartment. The lid was thick and heavy, but he could see nothing suspicious about it. He closed it again and fiddled with the raised letters, without result.

He had actually decided to replace the contents when a fresh thought occurred to him. *"The bee ascends!"* Feverishly Hornblower took hold of the "B" on the lid. He pushed it, tried to turn it. *"The bee ascends!"*

He put thumb and finger into the two hollows in the loops of the "B", took a firm grip and pulled upward. He was about to give up when the letter yielded a little, rising up out of the lid half an inch. Hornblower opened the box again, and could see nothing different. Fool that he was! *"Before my rolling eye."* Thumb and forefinger on the "I". First this way, then that way—and it turned!

Still no apparent further result. Hornblower looked at the poem again. *"Life still goes on within the heartless town."* He could make nothing of that. *"Dark forces claim my soul."* No. Of course! *"Strike 'em down."* That "'em". Hornblower put his hand on the "M" of "McCool" and pressed vigorously. It sank down into the lid. *"The sea will rise, the sea will fall."* Under firm pressure the first "C" slid upward, the second "C" slid downward. *"Turn full circle. Turn again."* Round went one "O", and then round went the other in the opposite direction. There was only the "L" now. Hornblower glanced at the poem. *"Hell will lift its head."* He guessed it at once; he took hold of the top of the "L" and pulled; the letter rose out of the lid as though hinged along the bottom, and at the same moment there was a loud decisive click inside the lid.

Nothing else was apparent, and Hornblower gingerly took hold of the lid and lifted it. Only half of it came up; the lower half stayed where it was, and in the oblong hollow between there lay a mass of papers, neatly packaged.

The first package was a surprise. Hornblower, peeping into it, saw that it was a great wad of five-pound notes—a very large sum of money. A second package also contained notes. There was ample money here to finance the opening moves of a new rebellion. The first thing he saw inside the next package was a list of names, with brief explanations written beside each. Hornblower did not have to read very far before he knew that this package contained the information necessary to start the rebellion. In the last package was a draft proclamation ready for printing. "*Irishmen!*" it began.

Hornblower took his seat on the cot again and tried to think, swaying with the motion of the ship. There was money that would make him rich for life. There was information which, if given to the government, would clutter every gallows in Ireland. Struck by a sudden thought, he put everything back into the chest and closed the lid.

For the moment it was a pleasant distraction, saving him from serious thought, to study the ingenious mechanism of the secret lock. Unless each operation was gone through in turn, nothing happened. The "I" would not turn unless the "B" was first pulled out, and it was most improbable that a casual investigator would pull at that "B" with the necessary force. It was most unlikely that anyone without a clue would ever discover how to open the lid, and the joint in the wood was marvellously well concealed. It occurred to Hornblower that when he should announce his discovery, matters would go badly with Payne, who had been charged with searching McCool's effects. Payne would be the laughing-stock of the fleet, a man both damned and condemned by everyone.

Hornblower thrust the chest back under the cot and, secure now against any unexpected entrance by Smith, went on to try to think about his discovery. That letter of McCool's had told the truth. "*Faithful unto death.*" McCool's last thought had been for the cause in which he died. If the wind in Tor Bay had stayed westerly another few hours, that chest might have made its way to Dublin.

On the other hand, now there would be commendation for him, praise, official notice—all very necessary to a junior lieutenant with no interests behind him to gain him his promotion to captain. And the hangman would have more work to do in Ireland. Hornblower remembered how McCool had died, and felt fresh nausea at the thought. Ireland was quiet now. And the victories of St. Vincent and the Nile and Camperdown had put an end to the imminent danger which England had gone through. England could afford to be merciful. He could afford to be merciful. And the money?

Later on, when Hornblower thought about this

incident in his past life, he cynically decided that he resisted temptation because bank notes are tricky things, numbered and easy to trace, and the ones in the chest might even have been forgeries manufactured by the French government. But Hornblower misinterpreted his own motives, possibly in self-defence, because they were so vague and so muddled that he was ashamed of them. He wanted to forget about McCool. He wanted to think of the whole incident as closed.

There were many hours to come of pacing the deck before he reached his decision, and there were several sleepless nights. But Hornblower made up his mind in the end, and made his preparations thoughtfully, and when the time came he acted with decision.

It was a quiet evening when he had the first watch; darkness had closed in on the Bay of Biscay, and the *Renown*, under easy sail, was loitering along over the black water with her consorts just in sight. Smith was at cards with the purser and the surgeon in the gun room. A word from Hornblower sent the two stupidest men of the watch down below to his cabin to carry up the sea chest, which he had laboriously covered with canvas in preparation for this night. It was heavy, for buried among the clothing inside were two twenty-four-pound shot. They left it in the scuppers at Hornblower's order. And then, when at four bells it was time for the *Renown* to tack, he was able, with one tremendous heave, to throw the thing overboard. The splash went unnoticed as the *Renown* tacked.

There was still that letter. It lay in Hornblower's writing case to trouble him when he saw it. Those tender sentences, that affectionate farewell; it seemed a shame that McCool's widow should not have the privilege of seeing them and treasuring them. But—but——

When the *Renown* lay in the Hamoaze, completing for the West Indies, Hornblower found himself sitting at dinner next to Payne. It took a little while to work the conversation around in the right direction.

"By the way," said Hornblower with elaborate casualness, "did McCool leave a widow?"

"A widow? No. Before he left Paris he was involved in a notorious scandal with La Gitanita, the dancer. But no widow."

"Oh," said Hornblower.

That letter, then, was as good a literary exercise as the poem had been. Hornblower realized that the arrival of a chest and a letter addressed to the Widow McCool at that particular house in Dublin would have received the attention it deserved from the people who lived there. It was a little irritating that he had given so much thought to the widow, but now the letter could follow the chest overside. And Payne would not be made the laughingstock of the fleet.

Ninety Days

Ebon G. Hardy, the president of the Pacific, Island & Orient Steamship Company, looked up at his capable secretary and said, "I want to think." Miss Hazzard threw her employer a glance at once quizzical and respectful, switched her desk telephone off, took her letter basket and withdrew. The big office was empty. Hardy dipped into a small drawer and fetched out a plug of tobacco. With a chew in his cheek he relaxed, closed his eyes and proceeded to solve the problem that confronted his line. He knew that no one dared disturb him till he rang the bell for Miss Hazzard.

For half an hour he made no movement. Then he opened his eyes, straightened up, got rid of his chew and summoned his force.

"Send for Captain Grey," he ordered his secretary.

To the chief bookkeeper he gave command to bring him instantly the month's accounts of the six vessels the Pacific, Island & Orient owned and operated. The cashier received directions to bring in all pay rolls. The chief stevedore gaped at a curt notice to stop loading the two steamers berthed at the company's pier.

Miss Hazzard replied to all queries from the harassed officials by stating, in firm tones, that she knew nothing of what had happened or would happen. To herself she recommended patience. When Ebon Hardy thought, officially and in the privacy of his own room, the Pacific, Island & Orient usually felt the effects for months. And till the final act was consummated few had any inklings of what the Old Man intended. So she even refused bustling Captain Grey a word of enlightenment, though he pleaded almost tearfully for some hint of what was in the air.

Behind closed doors Hardy opened converse with his general superintendent.

"Another three weeks will see this company on the rocks with all the other lines running on this coast," Hardy began.

"It's those agitators," Grey interrupted, reddening roots of his thick white hair. "If I had my way——"

"You've had your way for five years," Hardy said bluntly. "Don't interrupt! I have been spending six weeks on nothing else but the records of our six steamers. I discover, what I thought all along, that our property is deteriorating at the rate of thirty per cent a year. Our employees are down to fifty-five per cent of normal efficiency. Profits are sinking to nothing. And at this day and date freights haven't been higher in twenty years!"

Captain Grey's honest old eyes became piteous. "You fix the rates and make the schedules and give the orders," he responded huskily. "All I do is hire, fire and manage. I'm doing it just the same way I always did—and you never kicked before."

"I'm not really kicking now," Hardy remarked, fishing a cigar out and proffering it as a peace offering to the man who was his best friend. "But I've been thinking! That affair of the *T. J. Dawson* kind of stirred me up. It's the first time in our line a first-class skipper, a trustworthy engineer, and as good a mate as ever kept a ship, turned me down."

"It was the main feed pumps," Grey answered hastily.

"So I hear," Hardy retorted. "So you were told. So it was. And all that doesn't make a dratted bit of difference in the fact that the *T. J. Dawson* lay for six days within six hundred miles of San Francisco and called on the universe by wireless to tow her in. Feed me no more feed pumps, Grey."

"Archie Green, the engineer, has no superior on the Pacific, sir."

Hardy frowned. "That's exactly your attitude. Archie is a good engineer—and he comes to us with as paltry a tale of woe as ever dropped from the lips of drunken winch driver over a broken sling. Now you listen, Grey. I'm going to fire you—"for ninety days."

The general superintendent quietly picked up his cap and rose with dignity. But Hardy motioned him to his seat again.

"Ninety days, old scout! And you're not going out of here with a grouch on, nor to curse me, nor to sit and sulk where everybody can see you. You're going to listen to the words of wisdom from yours truly. Now——"

"Have done with your firing and lemme go!"

"I will not! If you say another word I'll fire Archie Green too. Now will you behave? All right. You have told me for six months, and I've read it every morning in the papers for five, that the trouble with us all is Labour Unrest with large fat capitals. You've come to me and told me So-and-So was reliable and So-and-So was unreliable—which meant that the first was satisfied with his job and the second grumbled. You got me to raise Captain Smith's monthly wages to three-fifty and you had me fire his son from being second mate of the *Harlow Hardy* because he talked too much. In other words, you've played the old safe hands for trumps, and ridden the talkative, dissatisfied ones to the rail and overside."

"You wouldn't have those rotten traitors running our ships?" Grey demanded hotly.

"They are running 'em," Hardy replied firmly. "Just at a time when we have no rivalry to fear, when there is more freight offered than double the number of vessels could handle, right when rates are in our own hands and profits heaped in the offing, our line goes to pieces from the inside. I have it all down here, each steamship and its crew, and I tell you the record is getting worse every day. Our employees have every bit of money they ever asked for. They can't make a demand we aren't ready to meet and make the freight pay for. And that's the time they go to bits, grumble, lose interest and wreck us. You might fire ninety per cent of our men and hire others in their place at double wages, and you wouldn't alter the fact. So you're fired for ninety days!"

"It's time!" the general superintendent said warmly. "High time, Ebon Hardy! Now all you have to do is to put some blasted loud-mouthed, empty-headed, half-baked radical labour agitator in my job and stand back and see the works go up in smoke."

Hardy looked down at his desk to conceal a smile. "And who would you recommend, Grey? Who is the man who answers that description? Didn't you say there was a youngster on the *Dawson* who was at the bottom of that trouble?"

"Milt Henderson," Grey returned savagely. "A young upstart with one of those confiding faces, a smooth tongue and a black heart. It's his kind that is wrecking lines like ours, with their everlasting sympathising with every man's little grouch and talking about what ought to be done and all that—as if ships were run for young fellows to hold their blamed talk fests on!"

Hardy nodded. "All right, Grey! Take ninety days off. Blocker will give you three months' pay when you go to his window. And keep away from our pier."

The ex-general superintendent stared, blinked, reddened and walked out stiffly. Hardy gazed after him affectionately, bit his lip, cursed softly and rang for Miss Hazzard.

"Get hold of Milton Henderson, second officer of the *T. J. Dawson*, and have him here in thirty minutes!"

The secretary took three minutes and then announced that Mr. Henderson would report as ordered.

"I want to think!" Hardy said, and was again left alone.

He had another bite off his hidden plug and closed his eyes. He opened them twelve minutes later and demanded Henderson.

The second mate of the *Dawson* walked in with a

kind of dogged defiance on his brown face, as if he were quite aware that he was a marked man and was up for a stiff time. Hardy scanned him shrewdly and not unkindly, motioned him to a chair and dismissed Miss Hazzard.

"I've asked all the questions I'm going to ask for ninety days, Mr. Henderson," the president of the Pacific, Island & Orient began quietly. "I know your record, where you live, your domestic affairs, your age, your weight and your condition of servitude. I know that you are friends with every man in our employ who is worth a darn. I know that you are at outs with the slackers and the weaklings. I know that you are conceited, egotistical and self-assured. You are the man for my money—for ninety days. I appoint you general superintendent of the line for ninety days at a salary of $600 a month. We have six steamships which you are well acquainted with, four hundred employees, and freight enough in sight to keep us busy for a year. Go to it!"

Henderson had listened with growing amazement. His habitual good-humoured expression had slowly absorbed the defiant one with which he had entered; now he looked puzzled, ugly.

"What's the joke, sir?" he asked.

"It's a big one," Hardy answered calmly. "I find that I can't run my ships with the old, steady, reliable men in charge. Times have changed. Eight out of ten men are not satisfied, no matter what one does for 'em in the way of wages, hours and bonuses. No company can make profits on twenty percent of its employees only. Captain Grey—as good a man of the old school as lives—failed trying it. I know you represent the eighty per cent. All right. The honest old twenty will flout you. Can you handle the other eighty and make good?"

"You—I begin to get you," Henderson said "You see——"

"I see nothing—except what I have told you," Hardy retorted. "I'm sick of sending ships to sea all shipshape and well found and loaded—and having 'em wireless in a day later from Lord knows where that they can't make port under their own steam. Go to it. You're the big boss."

Hardy pressed a button and looked up at Miss Hazzard. "Captain Henderson takes charge as general superintendent from this day," he remarked. "Make out the orders and have 'em posted." He swung on the bewildered youth.

"The *Harlow Hardy* and the *Dawson* are berthed for cargo. I stopped work on both. I don't care if they stick in port for ten days more, if need be. Load 'em and send 'em to sea when you're sure they'll arrive at the other end of the voyage. That's the only requirement I make. Any ship you dispatch which doesn't complete her voyage with uninjured cargo will be a mark against you."

Henderson rose. "This appointment is for ninety days?"

"From date."

"Hire and fire?"

"Anybody." Hardy glanced round. "Except my secretary, Miss Hazzard."

Henderson swallowed. "Right, sir. But you haven't gone far enough—if you want results."

The president opened his eyes slightly. "As how?"

"I want an assurance that you yourself will do as I say," Henderson answered firmly.

Hardy thought this over. "I see your point, Captain. You have the needful quality of gall, pure and unadulterated. I asked for it. I agree."

For twenty-four hours the Pacific, Island & Orient fumed, debated, complained and laughed over the new regime. Then it became known that the youthful superintendent held the distinctly unhumorous and non-debatable power of the purse. Attempts to see Ebon Hardy on the part of disgruntled employees were vain. Miss Hazzard brought out word that Captain Henderson was in charge.

The stranger in a high place did not act hastily or with much speech. He apparently forgot the manifold duties of his position as head of the whole line and devoted four days to the *T. J. Dawson*. He loaded her, put six new men on board her instead of five whom he transferred to other duties, held three minutes' heart-to-heart talk with Chief Engineer Archie Green, and sent her off on her voyage to Mazatlan. Then he took up the matter of the *Harlow Hardy*, half loaded for Honolulu, unloaded her, docked her, made certain repairs to her hull and assigned her six hundred tons more freight than any man had dared put into her within two years.

During this time a third steamer came in from Alaskan ports with a mixture of canned goods, concentrates and furs. After a cursory inspection of the latter portion of her cargo, Henderson quietly paid off her second and third officers, transferred her skipper—an old-timer in the company—to an easy berth ashore, and spent five precious hours with the engineer over lists of stores.

That evening President Hardy waited in his office, as he had been requested by his new general superintendent. When Henderson arrived, flushed but serene, his superior opened up on him promptly.

"Before we get to your business, Captain," he remarked curtly, "I want to know how it is that forty thousand dollars in furs consigned to Lark & Company were spoiled in six days?"

"I made a memo of that," Henderson replied. "When the *Homer Shaver* berthed I immediately went into the matter. You can't load concentrates and baled furs together and sweat 'em six days without hurting something. The concentrates came through uninjured."

"But what benighted imbecile ever loaded 'em together?" Hardy roared.

Henderson leaned back. "Hawkins was in command. He left it all to his mates, who don't like each other. Between them they got the mess started and Hawkins didn't have nerve enough to hang on two days more and straighten it out. He told me it would have cost him his job with Captain Grey."

"I see," Hardy answered. "But that doesn't alter the fact that the *Homer Shaver* made no profits on the voyage. Besides giving us a bad name."

"It won't happen again," Henderson said quietly. "I'm going to have the *Shaver* ready for cargo day after to-morrow."

"You put Captain Hawkins ashore," Hardy suggested. "Who have you got to go in command?"

Henderson grinned. "That's my business to-night. I looked round and I couldn't lay my hands on anyone fit to go as skipper. The voyage is to Hilo with that overdue sugar machinery, which is delicate stuff to handle."

"It is. And costly. The *Shaver* is really no vessel to dispatch with it. But I suppose there is no alternative. You must send the best captain you can lay hands on." Hardy rubbed his nose vigorously. "I suppose you have some youngster you met in a bar whom you've sent for to take her?"

"I have a man all picked," Henderson replied. "You."

Ebon Hardy rose from his chair as if lifted by some unseen cable. He stared at his young superintendent, started to speak, thought better of it, sat down, reached into the drawer for his plug and bit off an immense mouthful.

"Me?" he asked, in a muffled voice.

"You," Milt Henderson answered gravely.

"Will you please tell me why you pick the president of the Pacific, Island & Orient for the job of skippering a shabby cargo boat to the Hawaiians? Do you understand—oh, well! why do you say such things?"

Henderson leaned forward earnestly. "You jumped me into this position on three minutes' notice because matters were getting out of your control. You did it for a reason. At first I took it as a joke. But the harder I thought the less joke I saw in it. I'm going to make good—inside ninety days. And to make good I've got to land that cargo in Hilo on time out of the *Homer Shaver*. There isn't a skipper in our employ who can do it. You are my man. You'll go."

"Oh, I will, will I?" Hardy snorted.

"You promised me to back me up to the limit."

"I never promised to quit my job and make a fool of myself handling that *Shaver* packet. Not me!"

Henderson leaned back and smiled wearily. "All right! I thought so! D'ye really want to know what's wrong with this line? Why things are going to pieces right and left? Why ships depart and wireless for help? Why crews lag and bicker and listen to anyone who will tell them they are abused? You. You are the rotten spot in the apple. You're the sticking point. You're to blame for the troubles of the Pacific, Island & Orient."

Hardy narrowed his eyes and his jaws worked slowly on his chew. A slight significant flush mounted his face clear to his thinning hair. Men who knew the president of the line would have known that a thunderstorm was brewing. But Milton Henderson merely glared into those piercing eyes and waited.

Suddenly Hardy opened his lips and uttered a very quiet "Why?"

The strain was over. The younger man relaxed slightly.

"Because you sit here and plan things for other

men to put through, and then forget all the intervening steps and watch for results only."

"It's my business to look after policies, not details," Hardy reminded him.

"And the details are wrecking your policies."

"As how?"

Henderson threw out one hand in deprecatory gesture. "I've puzzled over how to tell you—how to make it all plain to you," he answered. "But it can't be done. Old Grey knew something was wrong and tried to bluff it through. It didn't work. The day of bluff is gone. That sugar machinery must be in Hilo in eleven days. A detail, Mr. Hardy, of course. But if that cargo doesn't arrive in eleven days—you lose. You've got no other ship to load it except the *Homer Shaver.* You have no skipper who will guarantee to get her across on time. And I can't explain to you why the Pacific, Island & Orient hasn't got that necessary skipper or the kind of men for a crew. But I can show you. I can teach you the bottom facts by sending you to sea as master of the *Shaver.* And when you have the chance to make good as president you turn me down. You won't go. You haven't the nerve. You quit."

Hardy reflected. "I quit? You insinuate that our employees are quitting on us because I quit—on them?"

"If you like to put it so," Henderson replied stiffly.

The older man smiled easily. "Why don't you take the steamer yourself, Captain Henderson?" Then he added: "If you need a real good man."

"I have other work to do," was the reply. "And less than: seventy days to do it in."

Hardy rose and took his visitor by the shoulder and thrust him toward the door. "I want to think," he rumbled. "Wait outside for me."

The superintendent left, with a shrug of his heavy shoulders, and Ebon Hardy took a fresh chew and seated himself and closed his eyes. He spent twenty minutes that way, roused up, opened the door and called Henderson in.

"I'll go skipper of the *Homer Shaver*," he said. "I'll sail as scheduled on Saturday, arrive in Hilo Sunday week, discharge and be back here nineteen days from my departure. I'll leave Miss Hazzard to manage my office while I am gone. I am probably a dratted fool and you will spill what beans aren't burnt to the bottom of the pot. But I'll go—and heaven help you when I get back!"

"Heaven help you to get back," Henderson replied solemnly.

He nodded and went out.

The next morning Hardy dispatched his routine business and called his secretary into private conference. He looked at her searchingly for a moment as she stood before his desk. He saw for the first time that she was extraordinarily good-looking, that she was well dressed, neatly shod, splendidly groomed. A little glimmer of approval shone in his eyes. Miss Hazzard, for the only time in her long experience with her employer, felt embarrassed. No personal note had ever been sounded in their relations.

"I'm going away day after to-morrow," Hardy announced. "You will take absolute charge in my absence." He paused. "I am going as captain of the *Homer Shaver* to Hilo with that cargo of sugar-mill stuff."

Utter incredulity shone in the girl's face. Then she nodded stiffly.

"You will stick to the routine, use your judgment—and steer clear of that smart young general superintendent, Milton Henderson."

"I'm not to interfere with him?" she asked formally.

"I wouldn't if I were you," Hardy responded. "He'd probably ship you to Guayaquil as stewardess of a hide-and-tallow boat. No, don't interfere with him. I'll want you here when I get back."

At noon entered Captain Grey, bristling. He had smashed his way through the outer office and a clerk hung anxiously to the skirt of his coat. He flourished a slip of paper.

"Look here, Hardy!" he blurted out. "You've got to act!"

"How dare you break into my office, you old fraud?" Hardy demanded in assumed wrath. "What is it, seeing you're here?"

The clerk vanished discreetly and the former superintendent flung the slip of paper under Hardy's eyes. He read it quickly. It was a wireless commercial message from the Pacific, Island & Orient steamer *Martha Rolls* and signed by her commander, Henry Tomlinson. It ran:

Messages sent you as general superintendent and to Hardy asking assistance answered by some understrapper who tells me no assistance needed and to make port under my own power. Abandon ship to-morrow morning if no assistance sent and notified.

"What the dickens does Tomlinson mean by relaying a dratted wireless to you—already discharged from the line?" Hardy asked quietly.

Grey ruffled his grey hair, swallowed and forced himself to clarity.

"The *Martha Rolls* left Balboa eighteen days ago

with general cargo for this port. I find Tomlinson reported his fuel-oil tanks leaking five days ago and his ship listed eight degrees to starboard. Your cub— your new superintendent wirelessed him back to never mind his tanks but hurry home with his freight."

"Well?"

Grey slapped the paper with his open palm. "Tomlinson and I were shipmates in the old days. A better seaman never stepped a deck. And you let him lie out there and cry for help and tell him to beat it on home! Naturally he sends me word of it—can't understand it! I come here and tell you your ship is going to be abandoned and you bawl 'Well?' in my ear. I won't stand it! When Tomlinson and his crew get in I'll back him up! I'll show all San Francisco what kind of an outfit the Pacific, Island & Orient is! I'll prove you let good ships and good skippers sink without help!"

Ebon Hardy scanned the paper again and glanced up at his belligerent caller. "Explain yourself," he said mildly. "What the dickens does a leaky fuel tank matter? He doesn't say he's out of oil, does he?"

Captain Grey stared, picked up the paper and laughed shortly. "The *Martha Rolls*—your own steamship—tanks leaking—and you look up and want to know what it matters! You're not fit to be head of this line, or any line, and I'm here to tell you so!"

Grey flung out, slamming the door behind him. Hardy looked over at his unperturbed secretary.

"Now there you are!" he grumbled. "Suppose I was gone and you in charge—what would you think?"

"I never did approve of sending steamers to sea on long voyages with old-fashioned tanks built against the outer plates," she replied coldly.

Her employer snapped a question, then another. He summoned a subordinate and demanded information. Then he got Henderson on the telephone.

When that official replied Hardy said curtly: "What about the *Martha Rolls*? Are you aware that her fuel tanks are built so that the ship's outer plates are one side of the tanks? Do you understand that when the oil leaks out water leaks in and raises heck with everything?"

The voice floated back with distracting calmness: "Yes, sir. I know all that. Do you?"

"But her fires are out, man!"

"I didn't send her to sea," Henderson responded coolly, waited and hung up.

Hardy stared at the telephone a long time. Then he laughed grimly, rose, and got his hat. At the door he turned to Miss Hazzard.

"I'm going down to the pier and have a look-see at the *Homer Shaver*. If I'm going to take her to sea I'd best be getting acquainted with her."

The secretary looked up with perfect composure. "What shall I reply to Captain Tomlinson if he wirelesses again?"

"He won't," Hardy replied curtly and strode off.

On the pier the watchman saluted the president respectfully and Hardy felt better. He went down the long shed amid the bustle and clamour of the working gangs till he came to a comparatively open space. Through the huge doorway in the side he saw the rusty flanks of the steamer berthed alongside. It was the *Homer Shaver*. He waited till a great mass of machinery had been safely swung from the pier, slipped by the panting men and to the gangplank. A moment later he was on the deck. A greasy overalled mechanic whom he recognized as the engineer started to push past him, looked, backed off and apologized.

"How's tricks, Mr. Harrison?" Hardy asked, reaching for a cigar.

But the chief merely nodded hastily and departed. Mr. Hardy felt snubbed. And he realized that in some way this employee resented his question. He proceeded forward along the saloon deck to the break, whence he looked down into the forehold.

What he saw fascinated him. He gazed long and intently. Then he hastened ashore, sought the chief stevedore and drew him aside.

"What the dickens do you mean by building all that machinery and stuff into that hold like the skeleton of a bridge? What's the idea? You're wasting space by hundreds of tons!"

The stevedore started to speak, remembered his position and smiled uneasily. "Oh, we'll stow her all right, sir. Leave it to me, sir. We're not finished!"

For the second time the president of the Pacific, Island & Orient felt the intended snub. He opened his lips to say something that would put this man in his place. But the stevedore was gone, his voice rolling out above the clangour of winches and rumble of trucks and whine of wire in sheaves. Hardy drew far into a shadow, leaned against a packing case, stopped a sweating labourer and asked for a chew. Having obtained this he sank back, closed his eyes and so remained till a shrill medley of whistles and bells told him it was noon. Then he returned to his office, transacted business in an abstracted fashion till four, called for his car and departed. The following day he spent but little time with Miss Hazzard, gave her some last instructions and bade her good-bye.

"Of course," the secretary said amiably, "I can

always get you by wireless if anything turns up that requires your personal attention."

Hardy smiled his relief. "Of course! Be sure and do so!"

The next morning Ebon Hardy went through the routine of enrolling himself as master of the steamship *Homer Shaver*, received the humorous and respectful remarks of officials with what geniality he could muster, and reported on the pier at ten o' clock, half an hour before the time set for his new command to sail for Hilo. He found Milton Henderson in the chartroom, talking with the chief mate. Hardy almost balked when he perceived that his reliance during the voyage was to be on a man whom he had lately discharged at Captain Grey's vociferous demand.

However, he shook hands briefly and said: "All right, Mr. Cable. As Captain Henderson has told you, I'm going master this trip."

The mate's jaw dropped. He glanced at the imperturbable superintendent, nodded distractedly and made excuse to be off.

"Now I've seen my chief officer," Hardy remarked grimly. "Who else have you picked?"

"You will take Ronald Anderson as engineer, Tackett as second mate, Rich as third," Henderson answered quietly.

Hardy blazed up "Every one of 'em a trouble-maker!"

"Who told you?"

Hardy swallowed his wrath and went to another question:

"Who is bos'n?"

"Mike O'Halloran."

"I'll be—well, what's the use?" the new commander of the *Homer Shaver* snapped. "You've picked a pretty lot of ruffians for this trip, and no mistake. But I'm going to make the voyage, as I promised. But you'd better watch out when I get ashore again!"

"I still have sixty days," Henderson answered, and proceeded with perfect calmness to lay down the law. "And you understand," he concluded, "that this line is not in the business of hiring tugs to drag its ships into port. I want no wild calls for help from you."

Hardy gulped his dignity and humiliated himself. "By the way, what did you do for Tomlinson?" he asked.

Henderson's keen eyes met Hardy's steadily. "Unless Captain Tomlinson wants to spoil the record of a lifetime he will berth the *Martha Rolls* four days hence right at this pier. He's too old a bird to be yelling for help when he isn't hurt."

The pilot arrived, soothed Hardy's feelings by

appearing duly impressed at the thought of the president of the Pacific, Island & Orient taking a ship for a trip, and gave orders that started the voyage. Henderson was the last ashore, shaking hands vigorously with Hardy, according to the immemorial custom of the sea.

Within ten minutes after *Homer Shaver* had backed out of the slip the superintendent was busy on another vessel and apparently oblivious of the fact that he had dispatched his superior to the outer ocean on a barely seaworthy steamer with a crew wholly undependable.

Miss Hazzard filed the history of the next six days in the form of slips of paper headed WIRELESS ex SS HOMER SHAVER, Vge 46.

Let us look over her smartly clad shoulder:

1. HENDERSON P I & O 10 am Oct 27
Hove to heavy sea restow cargo No 2 hold. One member crew hurt. Hope to proceed 9 pm if weather lightens. HARDY.

And this was the reply:

HARDY SS Homer Shaver 12.01 Oct 27
You are scheduled to arrive Hilo 6 am Nov 4.
HENDERSON.

2. HENDERSON P I & O 1 am Oct 28
Must return to port to land injured men unless
cargo can be restowed immediately. Heavy sea
and moderate gale. HARDY.

The reply ran:

HARDY SS Homer Shaver 4 am Oct 28
You are scheduled to arrive Hilo at 6 am Nov 4
without fail. HENDERSON.

3. HENDERSON P I & O 9 am Oct 29
Proceeding half speed. Heavy head sea. No 5
boiler leaking. HARDY.

Miss Hazzard gazed at the response to this
thoughtfully:

HARDY SS Homer Shaver 11 am
You are due Hilo 6 am Nov 4 this year.

HENDERSON.

4. HENDERSON P I & O Nov 2 8 am 9.15 am
10.10 am
Chief engineer reports low pressure head
cracked, No 5 boiler leaking, feed pump out of
order. Six members crew injured. Send tug from
Honolulu. HARDY.

The answer to this oft-repeated cry was brief:

HARDY SS Homer Shaver 12.01 pm Nov 2
Make all possible speed to port under your own power. All tugs busy other matters. Send six injured men to hospital if they live or to graveyard if they die.   HENDERSON.

5. HAZZARD P I & O S F 4 Nov 4 pm
Fire Henderson and get Grey back on job. Send tug from Honolulu assist me 150 miles east-by-south Koko Head. Notify all offices.

HARDY.

The reply to this was the neatest of the lot in typing:

HARDY SS Homer Shaver 6 pm 4 Nov
Former Superintendent Grey at sea as master SS Harlow Hardy. Henderson remains in charge. Directs you to make Hilo as ordered immediately, discharge cargo, turn over papers to resident agent and turn vessel over to Chief Officer who will take command. When your accounts are verified you will be free to seek other employment.

HAZZARD (Act'g for President).

6. HENDERSON P I & O 10 pm 7 Nov Hilo
SS Homer Shaver arrived 9 pm leaking badly, thirty degrees list to port, eight members crew injured. Will discharge cargo and proceed to Pearl Harbour to drydock.   HARDY.

The response to this was in the general superintendent's own script, crabbed but plain:

HARDY SS Homer Shaver, Hilo 9 am 8 Nov
Discharge cargo and proceed to San Francisco to drydock.   HENDERSON.

This was the history of the voyage which the *Homer Shaver* made under command of the president of the Pacific, Island & Orient Line. On the seventeenth of November Milton Henderson entered his superior's office and sought Miss Hazzard. She received him, as usual, with the composure of indifference. He came bluntly to his object.

"I haven't heard a word from the *Shaver* for four days," he told her. "Have you?"

Miss Hazzard looked critically at the point of her perfectly sharpened pencil.

"No."

Henderson sat down wearily. "You know," he

remarked conversationally, "that old packet was in no shape for the voyage."

"I believe Mr. Hardy cabled you that fact," she suggested.

"He did," the young man admitted, fixing his keen eyes on her face. "And I told him the truth—that we could allow him only eight days to make the trip home in, three in drydock and then two days to load again for Balboa. He sailed all right. If it were any other skipper but him I'd known where I get off. But—between you and me—I don't trust him."

"You mean you expect to see him turn up any fine morning without a word of warning?" Miss Hazzard answered with a faint tartness in her voice.

"I mean I'm darned near afraid he won't turn up at all!" The superintendent shifted uneasily in his chair. "You don't know all about my getting this job, Miss Hazzard. It was a kind of queer chance, I guess. And the first thing I knew I got interested. I've been with the Pacific, I. & O. for two years. I was about to quit the outfit when this happened. I admit I was in the dark a while. Then it got me. I wanted to show old Hardy and Grey and a few others how a line ought to be run. The only way to do that was to get Hardy out of the office and on a ship's deck. He came to the scratch pretty well, went off, and all that. I'll bet he learned a lot getting the old *Shaver* into port. But I stirred him up once too often. Now he's trying to go me one better and bring his steamer in on his own. I'm worried."

The secretary turned cool eyes on her caller.

"I possibly know more about your getting this position than you think," she remarked. "I happen to know that Mr. Hardy had been thinking a good deal about the way the line was going to pieces and preparing to try an experiment."

"But he'd never heard of me, except in passing," Henderson protested. "I heard how that happened. Old Grey mentioned my name because he'd been hauling me over the griddle not an hour before. Hardy simply grabbed at the name and sent for me. Then he couldn't very well back out—and here I am."

Miss Hazzard considered this dispassionately. "How could you expect Mr. Hardy to have a successful voyage when you gave him as officers the most unruly and dissatisfied men the line ever employed?"

Henderson flushed. "Those were good men," he insisted. "All they needed was handling right."

"He got into port all right."

The young man's face flushed more deeply. His eyes brightened. "It was fine work!" he burst out. "It was simply splendid. And that's why I feel so hanged rotten to think that Hardy is out there somewhere in a crippled steamer cursing me and trying to win home without a word or a whimper." He leaned forward earnestly. "Don't you see?"

Miss Hazzard studied her desk calendar with exasperating calmness. "I see that you still have forty-two days to be general superintendent of the P., I. & O.," she remarked.

He rose and smiled down on her. "I suppose you wouldn't feel equal to accepting my resignation?"

She shook her head decidedly. "I should not. You persuaded Captain Grey to take a ship, and there's really nobody left but you. I'm afraid you can't resign, Captain Henderson."

Their eyes met and something at once subtle and profound passed between them. Milton Henderson nodded.

"I have a notion," he said coldly, "that the whole trouble with Ebon Hardy was that he didn't know just who he had beside him in his office."

Miss Hazzard flushed faintly. A smile quivered at the corners of her mouth.

"You won't resign, then?"

"No. I reckon it's my business as general superintendent of this company to stick to my job and get the *Homer Shaver* home—and my boss back on the job." Henderson glanced thoughtfully at his watch, then at the lowering sky visible through the window. "South-east storm warnings were hoisted an hour ago all along the coast. Please call up the pier and order the *Washougal* to be ready with steam up in an hour."

Miss Hazzard obeyed. Then she adjusted her wrist watch, signed a few letters, received a basket of newly arrived mail and waited for her visitor to depart. But he sat at Hardy's old desk and stared into vacancy. At last she turned round and said with emphasis. "Did you really want the tug got ready for sea?"

Henderson looked up quickly. "Certainly."

He got to his feet and strolled over to her. There was an entire change in his manner. His voice was hard, businesslike and sharp. He spoke rapidly and clearly.

"Send a wireless every hour to the *Shaver*—broadcast it, and have other ships relay it—in these words:

"HARDY, S.S. *Homer Shaver*—Tug *Washougal* dispatched to your assistance at 4 p.m., seventeenth, with orders to cruise for small boats if need be.   —HENDERSON."

Miss Hazzard dotted the i's heavily, nibbled her pencil and asked, as if it did not matter really, "Who will take the tug to sea? Captain Ames?"

Henderson laughed roughly. "No man for the job at all. This is no harbour picnic."

She seemed to review in her mind the men who were possible skippers. Henderson initialled the transcript of the wireless he had just ordered sent, picked up his hat and said, "I'm going myself. Good day!"

The door had closed after him before Miss Hazzard could rise from her desk. She caught him in a hallway, where only an office boy sat. The superintendent heard her hurried "Captain, Captain!" and swung about in surprise.

"Yes?" he said civilly.

The secretary seemed at a loss. Her usual serenity was prodigiously disturbed. She glanced at him quickly. He took off his hat and looked at her doubtfully.

"The—what am I to do with any answers that we get from the *Shaver*?" she asked after several vain attempts to find words. "You know the tug has no wireless!"

"It has not," he replied. "One of the P., I. O's. little economies. But she's the only craft available, and I can't wait, you see."

"No," Miss Hazzard agreed, flushing; "you can't wait."

Henderson surveyed her thoughtfully. She looked

exceedingly wholesome, pretty and embarrassed. It puzzled him. This was surely not the young woman who had maintained the chill dignity of Hardy's austere office all these weeks.

"Good heavens!" he burst out suddenly. "It never entered my head!" He reached out and patted her arm clumsily. "Don't you worry! I'll have him safe ashore in ten days for you!"

Instantly she froze. She threw him a single look which made him withdraw his hand hastily as if burnt. Then she turned and went gracefully back to her office. Henderson went on his way, thinking of what an ass he had made of himself. Mingled with this sense of his own left-handedness was a profounder melancholy.

"Hardy is a bigger fool than I thought not to know the kind of girl in his own office. Lucky man!".

He sighed, and devoted his thoughts to the task ahead of him.

On the fourth day thereafter the tug *Washougal*, now very much the worse for wear, rounded to a quarter of a mile to leeward of the *Homer Shaver*, and her red-eyed, grey-faced skipper, Milton Henderson, helped launch a boat and soared off over the crested seas toward the wreck. His practised eyes took in the grim details swiftly.

"Just in time!" he murmured to himself.

After half an hour's jockeying under the dipping flanks of the disabled steamship, Henderson gained the deck and faced Hardy. The president of the P., I. & O. showed him an unshaven haggard countenance. But his voice was unshaken and his manner brusque as of old.

"Well?" he boomed at the younger man.

"I will pass you the pennant of my twelve-inch hawser," Henderson remarked huskily. "Can you make it fast anywhere?"

Both men glanced forward to the deeply sunken bows of the wallowing *Shaver*.

"Better make fast aft and tow us stern first," Hardy replied. "She may hold together a few hours."

Henderson nodded. "Send a wireless to the coast giving position and fact that the *Washougal* has hold of you," he said.

Hardy grinned. "No wireless, Captain."

"In that case," Henderson answered, with a responsive smile, "I reckon we better tuck into our job. The tug is not what I could wish."

"She was never built for this kind of work," Hardy returned. "What possessed you to bring her out here? You ought to have sent a full-powered steamer on this job."

Henderson shook his head. "The line has none to

spare. Anyway, it's up to me. I'll pull you in if you'll stay afloat."

"She won't," Hardy said briefly.

The superintendent's eyes flashed frostily. "I didn't come out here to keep your ship on top of the water, Captain. I came out to tow you in. Stand by to take my line."

An ashen-faced mate stumbled up, clutching at handholds.

"Better not wait too long!" he cried. "We've got to abandon ship inside an hour."

Hardy turned on him with amiable calmness, though his cracked lips quivered with weariness.

"We're going to take the tug's hawser and start in for the coast, Mr. Tackett."

The man gulped, glanced sheepishly at his superior and gathered himself together. He even raised his voice a note.

"Right, sir! Stand by to take a line!" He went off bawling hoarsely for his men.

Hardy looked intently at his superintendent, the man he had made on the impulse of a moment.

"I want you to understand that there isn't one of my officers who hasn't done three times what any dratted company has a right to expect of the best," he croaked. "And I'll sail hell with 'em any time!"

Henderson's face lit up. "They need you back in

the office," he said simply. "And I'm going to get you there!"

"It's a big two hundred miles!"

Henderson merely waved his hand and went back to his tug. At three in the morning of the fifth day the *Washougal* swung off the Pacific, Island & Orient pier, dropped back to her tow, cuddled under the *Shaver*'s side and nosed that almost submerged hulk tenderly in toward her berth. A freight ferry rumbling across the bay swerved with great splashings of paddle wheels, cries from the lofty pilot house and eloquent curses. Then she threw a searchlight beam across the obstacle in the fairway and withdrew, muttering amazement. Henderson felt the impact as the *Homer Shaver* nudged the pier, kicked his engines ahead to the extent of their poor power, floated clear and left the wheel. He had got his tow safely home. The *Washougal* drifted on up into the shadows of the slip and came to rest. Her commander rang his engines down and sank back on the sodden leather of the wheel-house. He relaxed and slept, his white face upturned to the stars that twinkled down through the shattered beams.

At nine in the morning President Hardy entered his office quietly, nodding this way and that to his employees, seated himself at his desk and summoned Miss Hazzard.

She came in without any variation of her usual civil "Good morning, Mr. Hardy," took her accustomed place, notebook on knee, and poised a neatly sharpened pencil.

"Take a letter to the general superintendent, Captain Grey," he said smoothly, and dictated:

DEAR SIR,

Please give the officers and crew of the S.S. *Homer Shaver* an extra month's pay apiece and shore leave from this date for six weeks on full pay. Notify all members of the crew to hold themselves in readiness to appear, if called upon, before the inspectors to testify as to the cause and nature of the damage incurred by the S.S. *Homer Shaver* during Voyage 46 from this port to Hilo and return.

Miss Hazzard completed this, murmured "Is Captain Grey superintendent again?" and proceeded, as though she had not asked the question: "Do you want this immediately?"

"Have it in type for me to sign right away," Hardy replied. "Call up the pier and ask Captain Henderson to step up here, please."

The secretary obeyed. Her employer glanced at her several times, caught a faint flush on the usually pale cheek and allowed himself a smile. When Henderson appeared, freshly shaven, bathed and dressed, Hardy motioned him to a chair, told Miss Hazzard to remain and said curtly, "You have still thirty-one days of the term we set for your employment as general superintendent. You will have thirty-one days' leave of absence on pay from this date. Captain Grey will take over your duties."

Henderson nodded indifferently and waited. Hardy stared at him, dropped his eyes to his desk, stirred impatiently and went on: "At the end of the thirty-one days you will come back to this office and take up the duties of vice-president and general manager."

The young man made no response to this.

He sat very quiet. It was evident that his thoughts were on another matter. Hardy watched him intently, frowned, looked round, got up and opened the door.

"I want to think," he told Miss Hazzard.

Alone with Henderson, who still seemed buried in a reverie, the president got out his hidden plug of tobacco, bit off a hearty chew and leaned back, with half-closed eyes. He remained thus for half an hour. Then he roused, got rid of his tobacco and pressed a button. Miss Hazzard returned, slightly flushed and without her customary cool composure.

"You will also take thirty-one days' leave of absence with full pay," Hardy told her.

Milton Henderson glanced up quickly, caught the secretary's startled eyes, blinked and looked at his superior. Ebon Hardy met that stare sternly.

"You think you are a very smart chap, Captain. I admit that you showed me a thing or two. But you have something still to learn. I refer you to Miss Hazzard—and the files of the wireless messages sent the *Hower Shaver*."

He rose, picked up his hat and walked out without further words. Henderson stared after him, then at Miss Hazzard.

"Now what——" he began.

She rose capably and drew from its place the little file of wireless slips and laid it silently before him. Henderson picked the sheets up one by one, studying them carefully. At last he uttered a startled exclamation. He laid an accusing finger on the one marked "5—Reply" and signed with Miss Hazzard's name in her own indubitable writing. He read it aloud:

Former Superintendent Grey at sea as master of SS Harlow Hardy. Henderson remains in charge. Directs you to make Hilo as ordered immediately, discharge cargo, turn over papers to resident agent and turn vessel over to Chief Officer who will take command. When your accounts are verified you will be free to seek other employment.

HAZZARD, act'g for President.

"You fired him!" he said solemnly. "Took it on your own responsibility to send a message I never saw! And he—he refers me to you!"

He gazed at her sternly.

Miss Hazzard's eyes shifted. She looked down, anywhere but at the young man who confronted her so gravely. Then her mouth curved slightly at the corners and her face was flooded with colour.

"It was the only thing to do!" she said unsteadily. "I—I wanted you to make him see you were master! I—I hate a man who can't carry a thing through! I—I thought you might not like to send such a message, so I—I sent it, anyway!"

Henderson surveyed her wonderingly. A curious decisiveness hardened his face. He rose and thrust the file away.

"You are quite right," he admitted. "I wouldn't have sent it. I'd ha' backed down at the last minute! You've taught me a lot. And we've thirty-one days for you to teach me the rest!"

Miss Hazzard recovered her poise and met his eyes calmly. "I'm afraid it will take you more than thirty-one days to finish your education, Captain Henderson!"

"Oh, make it thirty-one years and—ninety days," he replied rashly. "Starting with dinner to-night!"

She tried to stare his bold eyes down, failed—and took refuge in Eve's protest: "But I don't know you well enough!"

Henderson shook his head solemnly. "It took Ebon Hardy just fifty-nine days to get thoroughly acquainted with me. I'll allow you the full ninety. I'll call at six o'clock!"

The door opened and Captain Grey came in, like a gale. He stared round, saw Henderson and shook hands cordially.

"By ginger, you saved my life, Mrs. Grey tells me, by sending me on that voyage. It fixed my digestion up for another ten years. Where's Hardy?"

"On the pier," Henderson said promptly.

Grey nodded and brushed back his thick white hair. "Seems like he'll spend more time on the pier from now on. And two steamers in this morning with full cargoes two days ahead of time! Real action for our money!" he said.

"I want you to come down and straighten out things a little. Not that there's the least trouble—but you have the details down pat."

"I'm busy," Henderson returned briefly.

The superintendent stared, shook his head doubtfully and turned to Miss Hazzard. "Probably you know all about what I want," he suggested. "You usually do."

"She's busy, too," Henderson interposed firmly.

Captain Grey scowled, brightened up, smiled and prepared to depart.

"This always was a one-man concern," he remarked. "I seem to be the man this morning."

Ebon Hardy appeared in the doorway, saw Grey and said curtly, "I want to see you, Grey, about alterations on the *Shaver* while we're repairing her. I never knew before that——"

Their voices fell to a low murmur.

Henderson looked at Miss Hazzard and said, "Six, shall we say?"

She pressed the button that summoned her assistant, gave that young woman her instructions and lifted starry eyes to Henderson. He made a quick step forward, but Hardy's voice rose suddenly, arresting every movement in the office.

"You think Tacket unreliable? Man dear, he was a mate with me on the *Shaver*! I don't give a hang if he preaches that salvation comes only by destroying all ships and drying up the sea. I can use him! And you don't like Mike O'Halloran? You're crazy! He was bos'un with me! Listen, I want to tell you something: You stop ashore and give your orders in morning—and fire the men who don't carry 'em out before five p.m. If a man comes to work at eight and you don't fancy the colour of his hair at noon—you send him to the timekeeper. Ships aren't run that way. Look at me! I took the *Homer Shaver* to sea with not less than eight men I didn't have any use for. But the moment I got outside the Golden Gate I was up against the real fact: There was work for forty men, I had thirty-six. I couldn't hire any more nor fire the ones I had. I turned to and did the forty men's work with my thirty-six, including the eight I'd ha' fired if the *Shaver* had been the pier with a gate at one end. Now that's the secret of running a line: Don't hire and fire, but do the work you have to do with the men you have. And then show 'em all you know the job yourself and can tuck into it at a pinch and give 'em all cards, spades, high and low casino and the game, and still win.

"Now about those frames——"

Henderson edged toward the door. Miss Hazzard softly slipped out with him. They were unnoticed by the two men holding high debate.

They gained the door and turned, like children escaping from a schoolroom, glanced at the absorbed dictators of the P., I. & O. and fled.

Captain Grey's stentorian tones carried clear to

the elevator: "I tell you, those boys I have on the *Harlow Hardy* don't need any instructions from you. I'll bet you ninety dollars they bring her in shape-shape and on time."

"Clear out!" Hardy roared back. "I want to think!"

They saw Grey's bulky figure in the doorway, his white hair bristling. "Think, confound you! Think for ninety days, and you won't alter the fact!"

Captain Henderson and Miss Hazzard looked at each other shyly. He rang the bell with a firm finger.

"They can't alter the fact," he said, and turned his eyes on his companion boldly.

Permissions Acknowledgements

'Hornblower and the Widow McCool' by C. S. Forester reprinted by permission of Peters Fraser & Dunlop (www.petersfraserdunlop.com) on behalf of Cassette Productions Ltd.

'Three Skeleton Key' by Georges G. Toudouze was first published in English by *Esquire* magazine.